# Crossing

# Bilingual Press/Editorial Bilingüe

*General Editor*
  Gary D. Keller

*Managing Editor*
  Karen S. Van Hooft

*Associate Editors*
  Karen M. Akins
  Barbara H. Firoozye

*Assistant Editor*
  Linda St. George Thurston

*Editorial Board*
  Juan Goytisolo
  Francisco Jiménez
  Eduardo Rivera
  Mario Vargas Llosa

*Address:*
  Bilingual Press
  Hispanic Research Center
  Arizona State University
  P.O. Box 872702
  Tempe, Arizona 85287-2702
  (602) 965-3867

# Manuel Luis Martínez

Bilingual Press/Editorial Bilingüe
TEMPE, ARIZONA

ISBN 0-927534-80-0

Library of Congress Cataloging-in-Publication Data

Martínez, Manuel Luis.
    Crossing / Manuel Luis Martínez.
      p.   cm.
    ISBN 0-927534-80-0 (alk. paper)
    1. Illegal aliens—Mexican-American Border Region—Fiction.
    2. Teenage boys—Mexican-American Border Region—Fiction.
    3. Mexican-Americans—Fiction.   I. Title.
    PS3563.A73339C76   1998
    813'.54—dc21                     98-35881
                                          CIP

*Cover design, interior by John Wincek, Aerocraft Charter Art Service*
*Back cover photo by Molly S. Snodgrass*

**Acknowledgments**

I would like to thank the following people for reading my novel and for making the time I spent writing less lonely and even quite bearable. Bill Allen was my first editor and reader. His faith in my ability kept me going early on. Thanks to my family, my father Manuel and my mother Janie, and Eli, Debbie, Janet, and Steve. They actually read everything I write. Also thanks go to my friends Gene Suárez, Walton Muyumba, Darryl Brown, Cathy Bowman, Terrence Deagle, and Martin Lastra, all artists and creators in their own right. I also appreciate Karen Akins's hard work on my manuscript. She is truly an excellent editor. And thanks, Olivia, for your inspiration and patience while I completed this novel.

For Maria, Janie, and Olivia.

Migration is the failure of roots. Displaced men are ecological victims. Between them and the sustaining earth a wedge has been driven. Eviction by droughts or dispossession by landlords, the impoverishment of the soil or conquest by arms—nature and man, separately or together, lay down the choice: move or die.

Ernesto Galarza, Merchants of Labor

# Preface

Sᴀɴ Aɴᴛᴏɴɪᴏ Dɪsᴘᴀᴛᴄʜ       August 7, 1971

## ILLEGALS SUFFOCATE TO DEATH:
### *"No One Knows Their Names"*

Last week twelve illegal aliens were discovered dead inside an abandoned railroad car on the west side of El Paso. There has been no comment as to whether all succumbed to heat exhaustion, dehydration, or slow suffocation. According to El Paso Sheriff's Deputy Bernardo Ortiz this was an apparently botched labor smuggling attempt. "It's very common on the border here for 'coyotes' to take money from poor men and then load them up like cattle on a train headed for who knows where." This is the third time this year that such a grisly discovery has been made. None of the aliens has yet been identified. "They leave their identification behind in case they get caught by la migra. It's easier to lie that way. No one knows their names. No records in case they try it again later. They have to be careful, you know. They don't go throwing their names around. They remain anonymous." Ortiz could only guess at how long the men had been locked in the car. "It might have been only three or four days. It wouldn't take too long under the extreme conditions these poor fellows found themselves in." John Richardson of the Immigration and Naturalization Service commented that the INS cannot stop the ever-increasing tide of illegal immigration without more federal funding. "You're going to get more and more cases like this," he said. "More dead Mexicans than at the Alamo." Although the door to the railroad car had apparently been broken open from the inside, the police have yet to account for any possible survivors.

# Chapter One

The men were all there. We had been told to meet at nightfall near the railroad stop at the slaughterhouse in Monterrey. They stood waiting in a field. I walked toward them, stepping through the brush and around the small mesquite trees that crowded the stretch of land.

There were twelve, besides me. Many of them looked like criminals. They were dirty, seeming to me the kind of men who stayed at the cantinas all night drinking and causing trouble. I didn't want to talk to them, so I sat away from them, watching. They didn't act like ruffians. They were very quiet; some sat on the ground, a few even slept. Two men stood whispering under a small tree. They seemed to be the only men talking. I tried to hear what they said but could not make it out.

One of them was tall and well-built. I could see he had been a farmer or even a rancher. He wore a straw cowboy hat. On his belt I could faintly make out the name Alejandro. The other man was shorter but looked even stronger than his friend. He was dark, with a thin mustache and small ears. His hair was slicked back and he had a habit of spitting. I heard Alejandro call him Pablo. He said something into Pablo's ear and laughed, but the shorter man didn't react. He seemed to be appraising the other men, measuring them against each other. Alejandro said something again, and Pablo nodded sharply. "You," he said, pointing at me, "get over here with the rest." I moved closer to the other men. "Don't bother making any good friends. You won't have time. And keep your mouth shut."

Then I noticed the old man. He sat alone, like me, slightly apart from the rest of the men. I couldn't make out his face, but in the dim light I could see he had only half of his right hand.

We waited for Rosales, the labor contractor. When he got there he took our money and told us we were to be silent until we got off the train. He had three men with him, one of them wearing a federal uniform. I don't know if he really was one or not. I didn't think a federal would get himself mixed up in such a thing as this. Rosales told me it would be a difficult journey.

"You won't like the train, boy. It gets very difficult. Hot. Men get ill-tempered. You see that old one over there?" He pointed to the man with the mutilated hand. "He's too old. He'll probably die. Does that scare you? To know you'll have to ride in the boxcar with a dead man?"

"No," I said, "I've seen dead men before in my village."

"Well, we'll see. You're young. How old are you anyway?"

"I'll be seventeen at the end of the year," I told him, fearing he would think me too young for the trip.

"Well, you look strong. I think you helped your father on a farm." He smiled, exposing a mossy set of teeth. "Your shoulders are broad. You'll be able to carry large sacks of fruit and such. I think you'll do very well." He stroked my shoulder. I drew back. "Then again I don't know for certain. Stronger men than you have failed to survive the trip. Many have gone mad in the darkness or from thirst. How you comport yourself within those walls means everything. You're going back to the womb." He smiled again, this time with anger in his eyes. "You must pay me now, just in case."

I handed him two hundred thousand pesos, which he took without counting.

"The rest you work off. It won't take a strong boy like you very long. Now remember, when you get into the box, don't make noise. You must all be silent." He smiled again. "You do want to go to Texas, right?" He then collected the rest of the money from the other men, and after telling one of his companions something privately he left.

For the next hour or so we walked. I did not know where we were. I thought of my mother. She had begged me not to leave. The night before I left, she had cried. "You don't have to leave, mijo. I want my handsome boy here."

She held my face in her hands, and for a minute I knew I should not leave. I weakened. "I know, Mamá. I'll stay. I won't go. I won't go." But as the words left my mouth I hated her. I felt like shaking her hands from my cheeks and running.

Her face brightened at my surrender. "I knew my boy wouldn't leave me alone. Since your birth I knew you would always be here for me. You're my handsome, dark boy. Every day you look more like your father." She ran her fingers over my hair.

I left that night after she fell asleep. I had to go. Ever since my friend Jorge had told me of a man who would provide a job and transportation to Texas, I had begun to save and plan.

"Yes, Luis, we'll go together. This man told me that in Texas we can go on the piscas. We pick cotton in Texas, then go to California for grapes. In Michigan we pick tomatoes. He told me that in Texas there's a lot of gente. 'If you get into trouble, there's always someone to ask for help. Every one of those Texas towns has a barrio. All you gotta do is walk around till you find it.' He says when he was there he was young and stupid like us and he found friends who showed him where to go and what to say to get work. My tío, he's never gone, but he has friends who've made the trip, and they said Texas was the best place to start. We'll find a place to live, maybe we can even get one or two other men to live with us. That way we can afford to send more money home. We'll learn inglés like that cabrón Ernesto who went to California a few years ago. We'll go, right?"

I agreed readily. Even though we disliked Ernesto, it was an opinion rooted in envy. He had already gone to the U.S. and found work as a machinist. He sent money home and his sisters would sneak over to see him, always coming back with good clothes and enough money so their parents wouldn't have to work as hard. Ernesto had come back two years before, wearing a gold wristwatch and spectacles that looked expensive. He told everyone he had his own car in Los Angeles and described the highways and tall buildings. When one of the old men told him that Los Angeles sounded like Mexico City, he laughed. "It's nothing like Mexico City. In 'Elay' everything works right. You don't have a bunch of kids hanging off the back of every bus. The cops there keep order. It's true they don't like Mexicans or blacks, but things are orderly. You can get anything to eat any time of night or day. They have movie theaters everywhere and you can choose from dozens of flicks. That's what they call them there. You can even watch the corny Mexican stuff if you want." Ese cabrón se cree muy americano, went the gossip around our village. That didn't deter us. From then on, Jorge and I began to plan our own move al norte. But in the end only I went.

Jorge came over the morning I left. He couldn't say what he wanted to say. He wanted to say he was ashamed and he knew he was a coward, but he only wished me luck. He tried to give me a few pesos but I turned them down.

"Look, Luis, take them. You can pay me back when you start making money in Texas."

"I won't need pesos in Texas. They don't take those there. There they have real money. There you get paid and you get paid American money."

I refused to use his name. When he said goodbye, I nodded but didn't shake his hand. He left. I felt sorry for him because I knew he would never leave this little village, and I was going.

*    *    *

Soon I could smell the sweet-rotted stench of the stockyard and knew we were near the place where the train would pick us up. When we were in sight of the tracks, the man dressed like a federal told us to stay back.

Within a few minutes a train pulled into the stockyard. The train was very long. I could not see the end of it. It seemed to stretch endlessly into the darkness. The federal waited a few minutes until a man on the train got off, then went to him. They talked for a few seconds and then the man got back on the train. I became scared that something had gone wrong and that we would not be going after all. But then the federal waved to Alejandro and Pablo.

"Shut your mouths and follow us," Alejandro said. They led us to one of the cars near the end of the train. It was a large wooden boxcar. They unlocked the large door, sliding it open noisily. The screech made us hover nervously around its mouth.

"Pendejo," cried Pablo. "Do you want someone to hear?" He turned toward us. "Hurry up, you idiots. And remember you all have to keep your mouths shut."

As the men started to enter the car, Rosales took Pablo and Alejandro aside, explaining something to them in quiet tones. Neither said anything in reply, although they nodded often.

As we filed up to the entrance I strained forward, trying to glimpse inside the chamber in which I would ride to my freedom. The old man stood behind me.

"You seem very anxious to enter," he said. "Don't get too excited now; I think you may be in much more of a hurry to get out by the time it's over."

I did not say anything. I only craned my head farther.

"It's not such a bad idea to look now," the old man continued. "You won't see anything once they close those doors."

A lightpost hanging in front of a tool shed threw a dim light into the car. Most of the interior was in shadow, but I could make out a haystack in the center of the floor. In one of the corners stood a small metal barrel.

The man in front of me climbed in. I stood in the doorway for a moment, unsure.

"Ándale," someone snarled from behind me. I slowly lifted my knee onto the floorboard of the car.

"Go on," the old man said gently. He put his hand under my arm as if to lift me up.

I pulled away roughly.

"I can do it myself," I said, and then I jumped quickly inside. The floor was made of old unpainted wood. It creaked as I made my way to the farthest corner. I threw my bedroll down but did not unroll it. I sat on it instead and leaned against the wall, which was made of rough, splintered wood. It had been painted, but long ago. The paint had come away in large strips, exposing ancient planks.

The old man sat down against the same wall, about ten yards away. The rest of the men sat as far away from each other as possible unless they had come together, so that all four walls had men leaning or sitting against them.

"This barrel has water in it," said a long-haired man, tapping the barrel with his finger.

"Leave that alone," said Pablo, climbing into the boxcar. Alejandro followed him inside. "That's for later. I'll tell you when." The long-haired man pulled his hand away from the barrel and sat down without a word.

After everyone was in the car, Rosales's men slid the door shut from the outside. We all listened as they latched and then padlocked it. The click of the padlock echoed in the darkness.

# Chapter Two

The men had been very quiet as we waited for the train to start. When finally it did move, they began talking. My eyes had adjusted to the darkness, but all I could see were pale streams of moonlight coming through the cracks in the ceiling. I could hear two men discussing the trip.

"How long do you think it will take? I don't like riding in this box like a cow. Rosales told me we would be in Texas in twelve hours and then on to the Valley by tomorrow night."

"Well, Chico, we're no longer able to tell. Que Dios nos bendiga."

I tried to keep from falling asleep. I felt that the moment I fell asleep I would die, but it was hard to keep my eyes open. It was very dark in the boxcar. I could hear whispering from all directions. "Sssst, sssst, sssst." The darkness seemed to take me, to hide me. I imagined that all the whispers were evil spirits looking for me. I was blind in there, as if my eyes were shut tightly, yet my eyes were open, and I was afraid.

I began to think my uncle had been right. He had been opposed to the trip. At first he had even refused to take me to Monterrey, and he cautioned me about Rosales.

"You think you know what it takes to do well in el norte. All you've heard is that braggart Ernesto telling his tales about big cities and women. It's all fantasy. You've never heard of Jesse Galván. He went with a man like Rosales who promised to get him into America to work. That pendejo spent a month waiting in Nuevo Laredo, sleeping in a shit-hole with a bunch of other pendejos. What's worse is that he'd already given all his money to the man who told him he'd get him to Texas. Jesse waited until his stomach couldn't take any more hunger. It's the stomach, not the heart, that tells you when it's time to move on. Don't let anyone fool you. He got hungry enough to leave the shack where he was wait-ing. He got lost in Nuevo Laredo and couldn't make his way back. I don't know if that malcriado ever returned for those poor fools, but Jesse wasn't there if he did. He walked around all night until, scared as he was, he decided to cross over on his own. That poor fucker, he walked right across the bridge during the early morning hours. Can you imagine, him dirty and smelling like he did, looking like a campesino who's been sleeping in shit-laden pastures, thinking he wouldn't be spotted? Those gringo border guards, they grabbed him and dropped him on the Nuevo Laredo side with a couple of kicks in the ass and a warning that next time he did some-thing so stupid, he'd get a professional "wetback's beating." He had to come back to the village with nothing. His shoes were as worn out as his pride when he wandered in, thin after the long walk. He told me he had lived on roots and a few carrots he'd stolen from a vegetable cart in Laredo. Imagine that. There was no 'Elay' for him. There's all kinds of people out there waiting to take the few pesos you have in your pocket. They know your dreams keep you from seeing through them. They'll rob you blind. Maybe so blind you won't be able to find your way back here again."

But he saw that I had made my mind up to go. I didn't have to say anything more to convince him.

It took me the whole night to walk to his house, which had once sat next to a pasture where he had kept a small herd of cattle. Now there was nothing but a dry dirt lot. The cattle had been diseased. He burned the carcasses rather than sell fouled meat.

I found him the morning of my departure sitting in front of his house. He looked like my father. His hair was dark and straight, his eyes black and tightly squinted from the sun. His skin was now very dark, having been burned by the sun for forty years. As I walked up to where he sat on the porch, I could feel his surrender. His once strong, proud shoulders, so much like my father's, now sagged. His jaw drooped, and lines of weariness obscured the fire, the life that had once lit his face. I could not look into his eyes.

"So you will go?" he said.

I nodded my head.

"So much like your father," he said. "You look very much like him right now." I sat down next to him. "Did you know that once, when the mines were still alive, he was almost killed? It was before you were born. Before he met your mother. We were little more than children, me and your father." His speech slowed as he saw himself as a young man again. "We worked like dogs at that mine. Sometimes we started long before the sun came up. The sun doesn't matter in a mine. We went into the mountain when it was dark and worked for sometimes sixteen, even twenty hours. Then we came up from the darkness into the darkness of the night. There were weeks upon weeks when we didn't see the sun. It became a memory, a much loved but unseen friend. Only the lanterns and dim bulbs reminded us of the brilliance of el sol.

"After weeks of living in darkness, we would be allowed to work a short day. Sometimes we had a week of short days. I'll never forget your father saying, '¡Fernando, ahora vemos el sol! Today we see the sun!' We would come out of the mountain into the sunlight.

"When we first came up I would always close my eyes because the light seemed to burn into them, but your father would look up wide-eyed, greeting the sun. Light was what he lived for, I think. But we had no choice. We had to live in darkness if we were to eat.

"Then we were told we would always have to work during the day unless we paid the jefe a bribe to let us work at night.

"Your father didn't pay. He continued to come to work during the night and worked his full shifts. The boss learned of this. He threatened your father, but still your father came at night.

"After a week, he changed to days. Everyone thought he had given up. But not so. After a week of days he started to come for the night shift.

"The boss waited. He didn't threaten your father again. I think he was afraid of him. Your father was becoming the leader. He was more the jefe than the jefe was. One evening after work, your father confided in me that the boss had offered to make him supervisor of the night shift if only he would stop disobeying the rules. I don't know, Luis, maybe he was tempted. He was a young man in those days. But he didn't accept the jefe's bribe. 'So the men can call me Judas?' he told him.

"The next night, your father was working with a small group of men in one of the older veins when three strange men appeared in the cave. One of them struck your father in the back of the leg with a pick-axe. It happened very quickly. His crew stood back, afraid, as your father fell to the ground. Then the three strangers left, saying, 'You'll die in the darkness, cabrón! You'll never leave unless you do what the jefe wants. He has the power. Do what he wants or we'll be back.'

"Your father was sick for many days. The muscle in his thigh had been severed. Since you've made the decision to leave, maybe it's better that you know this about your father."

It was time to leave now, and I walked off the porch to the truck without looking back to see if my uncle was following. I put my quilt, which I had rolled around my canteen, into the back of his old truck. "I'm ready," I said.

My uncle nodded, getting into the truck. We drove to Monterrey in silence. I watched the mountains looming before me, seeming very close yet always in the distance.

It was dark when we got to Monterrey. The factories were closing, the many people rushing home.

"You could get a job in one of these factories, Luis. Monterrey is not so bad."

"You know," I said, "that I don't know the right people here. The streets are full of beggars who thought they could get a job in Monterrey."

He said nothing else to dissuade me. At nightfall we said our goodbyes. I asked him to watch over my mother until I could send her some money. He agreed, wishing me God's help. I walked away slowly. Doubt began to cloud my mind. For a moment, I almost turned back toward the truck, hoping my uncle would tell me not to go. That is all it would have taken for me to return to Bustamante. I think he sensed that and so left quickly. As I heard the truck start up, I panicked. It took everything I had to continue walking toward the darkened field.

\* \* \*

Slowly the whispering died down. I heard a snore from one corner, and then another. In the darkness it reminded me of my father's snoring. I remembered how, only a month before he died, he had taken me into the mountains to see the deserted mines that surround Bustamante.

We spent all day climbing up the highest mountain. The trees were short and thin, and the rocks were unsteady, sometimes rolling as I tried to put my foot on them for leverage. My father stayed a few feet behind me saying, "Ándale, Luis. Come, Luis, climb, don't watch your feet. Look up, up . . . up . . . that's right, up. Lean forward and strain. You must strain."

It was nightfall when we reached the top. The cold mountain air was blowing softly yet crazily, one moment from the north, the next from the south.

"The wind changes direction fast up here, doesn't it, Luis?" asked my father.

I nodded. I was awestruck as we sat at the edge of a cliff. My father had built a fire to warm us. Neither of us talked as we stared into its flames.

As the fire died down my father continued to look at the glowing embers and began to speak. "You must never forget who you come from, Luis. The past is like this mountain, immovable, irrefutable. It stands here for all to see. Whether you wish to acknowledge it makes no difference. It is here. Your people have been here as long as this mountain. They saw the sun in its beginning, as now you see it at its end. Look," he said, pointing at the moon, large and yellow, glowing softly in the sky. The stars shone behind it, old yet new. I looked at my father. He stared at the sky, lost in its beauty. His face was intent, serious, more so than I had ever seen. "No matter what happens in this world, this mountain remains. No matter what happens to you," he said, still looking skywards, "like this mountain, your people remain. In your memory, in your soul, in your very blood and character."

That night we slept in a shallow cave that had been used as shelter by some long-dead miner. My father and I lay on the ground in quilts we'd bought in the mercado in Bustamante. As I heard my father begin to snore, I looked out from where I lay, through the opening in the cave, at the stars my father had contemplated so thoughtfully. I could not understand.

In the train, as I heard those men snoring, I longed for stars to appear in the blackness of the railroad car, but they did not.

*   *   *

That night I slept very little. I would wake up suddenly, thinking of my mother, my uncle, my father, my little brother Benito. I dreamt of my mother.

She was alone in our small house. She sat on the chair my father had made when I was only ten. She said nothing, forlorn, gazing uncertainly at the floor. When she lifted her face, it was white, with dark circles around her eyes. Her face grew whiter and whiter, the circles slowly taking the place of her eyes. She said nothing, only stared. Darkness encircled her, fear crowding her face. I jerked awake, moaning very loudly. I felt like standing and breaking through the door, jumping from the train, and making my way home. My own mind became treacherous. I began to fear that my mother would be dead when next I saw her.

What if that is God giving me a warning that my mother is dying? I covered my ears, trying to shut out my thoughts, but it did no good. The chair, the chair, oh God the chair, remember the chair, the damned chair. No! The good chair, my father made the chair, the chair, remember how we made the chair? No, mother could be dead! No, no, no. Remember the chair and how Papi made it. The time he took you to cut a tree, a special tree, one that could hold the stress.

"Pick an oak. A nice fat one. You see that one over there, hiding behind the pecan tree? He knows it's his day to become something."

I saw my father in the darkness, the memory forming before my eyes. I saw him let me take a few futile chops at the trunk. He watched me, smiling.

"That's it. That's it. That's the way you cut a tree down to size."

My hands began to hurt, but I kept on chopping. A blister began to form near my thumb, but still I would not stop. My father watched from behind. I could feel him staring at me.

Then he said, "Luis, that's enough. You've given me a good start. A very good start. I'll use the recess that you've made as the wedge."

I watched him chop at the tree for hours. Then slowly the tree began to lean—then a snap, like a bone was breaking, then many bones. The tree came rushing down, meeting the ground with a thunder clap.

"You see what your little wedge did? That's what determination does. If you decide to do something and you put your strength into doing it, even a little thing becomes great."

We took the wood home to make planks. The next day I could barely move. My arms ached, my shoulders felt as if every movement was slowly ripping them in two. But still I helped my father make the chair for my mother. I watched as he sanded the new planks and carved decorations on the legs. I sat for hours, fascinated with my father's labor. When it was finished he sent me to get my mother. I took her by the hand into the workroom.

My father stood behind the chair, smiling. My mother sat in it.

"Oh, how beautiful, Pedro. So strong too," she said.

My father nodded at me, and I smiled, feeling that I had helped make my mother happy.

But in the darkness of the train, it all seemed so far away, and I suddenly understood that it really was all very far away. My father was dead, my mother in Bustamante, my old life gone, a new one not yet started.

\*     \*     \*

The train stopped a short while later. I could see tiny rays of daybreak drifting down through the cracks, shedding a dim light. My eyes adjusted and I could make out shapes. Some men were awake and whispering. I could sense relief in the way they moved and in their animated whispers. I too was relieved that the first night was over. I prayed that we would not have to spend another in the box.

But soon what had been warm during the night became a sweatbox. As the morning gave way to day, the air in the boxcar assaulted us. Men began to drink the water rapidly.

The old man watched, still sitting. "You shouldn't drink the water so quickly. You'll only suffer later. Don't be fools. This water must last us until we get to Texas."

"Old man, you worry too much," said Pablo. "Rosales told us we would be in Texas by nightfall. Why should we suffer now? If you want to save water, don't drink any. When you die of thirst, we'll bury your wrinkled, gray corpse under the bale of hay."

# Chapter Three

Now the heat had reached its peak. Some of the men were panting. The train had been still for a long time, which seemed to make the car even hotter. I was sweating badly. I tried very hard to stay still; every movement sent a wave of heat through my body.

My grandmother used a large stone oven for baking pottery. I would take the soft clumps of clay to her potter's wheel, and she would peddle the wheel as her large hands touched here and there, producing a pitcher or vase. I would carry them one by one to the oven. As she swung open the large door, a wave of heat would storm over me, almost knocking me down. I felt trapped in those waves of heat, hardening, my form fixed.

\*    \*    \*

Soft moans filled the air, seeming to make it hotter. I felt like screaming at them to shut up. Only the weariness that pinned my body against the floor kept me from doing it. I was sleepy, but sleep came for only a few minutes at a time. Then I would awaken from one darkness to another.

I did not try to take any water. The men had only one cup, and they were beginning to accuse each other of keeping it too long. A fight broke out between a Guatemalan and a small man called Chico.

"Indio," Chico spat at the Guatemalan, "give me that cup. I don't want your Indian mouth to pollute the water."

The Guatemalan did not respond. Instead he dipped the cup back into the barrel and drank slowly.

"Didn't you hear me? ¡Indio cabrón! Give me that cup or I'll take it from you."

The Guatemalan paid no attention. He dipped the cup back into the barrel, lifting it once again to his mouth. Chico stood there watching, his fists clenched, breathing rapidly. "You pinche Guatemalteco. You don't even belong here. You people take everything when you come and leave nothing. You shouldn't be here." He turned to the men who were hunched in the darkness. "He shouldn't even be in here with us." He gestured toward the Guatemalan. "He'll drink all the water if we don't stop him."

A voice I recognized as belonging to Chico's companion said, "It's too hot to fight. Let him finish."

Instead Chico slapped the cup from the Guatemalan's hand. The Guatemalan struck him in the face with his elbow. I heard a muffled snap as Chico grabbed his own bloody face. The Guatemalan kicked him in the groin and Chico doubled over, collapsing onto the floor.

No one moved. Chico stayed on the floor, doubled up like a baby. His friend just stood there looking down at him. The Guatemalan sat back down against the wall. Then I noticed the old man. He seemed to be staring at the door, as if dreaming. I decided then that I too would divorce myself from whatever happened in the box.

I sat still, trying to drown out the sound of the men greedily slurping the water. They were being careless, spilling it as they drank. Others even poured cupfuls on their heads, trying to cool themselves. But it did no good.

I began to get very thirsty, but I did not want to go to the barrel because I thought it would cause trouble. I thought about my canteen but did not drink from it for fear that one of the men would take it from me.

The canteen had been my father's. It was old and green, like an olive, and made of metal. On one side was a dent my father had made. The story of the dent always changed. Sometimes it had saved his life when an angry neighbor took a shot at him during a dispute about a fence. Once he told me he had used it to defend himself against a wolf he had surprised as he walked home from his job at the mine. My favorite tale of the canteen was the story he told of his youth when he and my uncle had left home for Mexico City to find better work. The canteen had gone the entire way with him. "I'd use it as a pillow at night by wrapping my spare shirt around it, and during the day we'd take rests along the road and drink from it. The dent I put there with my knotty head." My mother told me the dent had been made when he fell out of a tree. In bringing it on my journey, I hoped the canteen would bring me good luck and protection.

I waited for another hour, then could no longer stand the thirst. I got up slowly. I felt dizzy, as if I was going to faint, but I fought it. I staggered to the barrel. The train lurched as it began to slow down and I fell face first onto the floor. I lay there for a while, not having the strength to push myself up. Then I felt someone shaking me.

"Boy, boy?" I heard the old man say. "Can you hear me? You'd better get some water. You'll die if you don't."

I felt him stand up and walk off. He returned with a cup of water. "Drink this," he said. "It's very warm, but it'll do. Drink it."

The water tasted of the rust that polluted it, but as it rushed down my throat, I could remember nothing better that I had ever tasted. "Thank you," I said.

"Don't thank me," said the old man. "Next time don't be such a fool. Drink the water. Do you think any of these animals will give you drink? They don't give a damn whether you live or die. You have to do that now."

I stood and walked to the barrel. I took the cup and drank until my stomach felt bloated. I brought the old man a cup of water, which he drank slowly.

"My name is Luis," I said. "I'm from Bustamante." I shook his hand.

"My name is Berto," he said. "I'm from nowhere. It's just south of everywhere."

His answer puzzled me, but I retrieved my bedroll, with its hidden canteen, and sat down next to Berto.

"Well, Berto from just south of everywhere, thank you for the water."

"As I said, save the thanks and learn to take care of yourself. You won't make it out of this goddam box if you don't." He said all this without anger.

I leaned back against the rough wall of the boxcar and closed my eyes, although in the dark it made no difference.

"Well, Luis," he continued, sounding now as if he wanted to talk, "tell me, how will you ever survive picking fruit in the hot sun if you don't have the sense to drink water when it is so close?"

"I'll do it the same way that a man with only half a right hand can pick fruit fast enough to survive."

"That is a very good answer," said Berto, "very good. But I must confess I don't know that I can pick fast enough to survive. We'll both hope."

# Chapter Four

When I awoke, the train was moving again.

"The worst of the heat is over for now," Berto said. "The heat has an edge to it. When you feel the edge, it's best to get out of the heat if you can. I trace much evil to heat. The gringos don't understand the siesta, Luis. They believe that the Mexican is lazy, that he uses it to sleep or to lay with his wife, but it isn't so. The heat can make a man crazy, crazy enough to kill. I think we may see that before we arrive in Texas."

"Crazy, how?" I asked. He said nothing for a moment. "My father made barrels in our village in Jalisco when I was a boy. But when a factory in the north began to make them, there was no longer any need for his labor. After a while, he made only a few repairs for neighbors. He sent word to my cousin in Veracruz that he would like to apprentice me to him. His name was Julio, and I had heard my father speak of him as a successful exporter of cloth. I didn't want to go, but you see, there was no choice. My mother didn't dare oppose him openly. Instead she told me that I would come home soon and that I must learn from Julio and return a success. I knew nothing of success and did not want to go.

"On the day I left, my father didn't allow my mother to see me off. 'You mustn't make him weak,' he told her as he ordered me outside. When he climbed on the wagon he told me to look upon his home for the last time should I disgrace him. I felt sick riding beside him through the rolling, golden hill country that surrounded my village. Its curves seemed to me right then to be as comforting as my mother's breasts, hiding places for me to run to and wait for this plan of my father's to wither away. The irony is still bitter for me, that I was leaving the state where Don Hidalgo had ended slavery for our people, to go to Veracruz, where Cortés, el diablo original, had begun his conquest.

"I believe my father felt some guilt as night met us on our ride east. 'There's ocean in Veracruz as well, boy. It's not as beautiful as the water of Careyes, but at least you won't be lonely for the breezes or smells of la playa.' Our village was only half a day's walk from the beaches of Careyes, where my father would take my mother to visit her people. I had enjoyed those trips, walking with my cousins to the steep, tree-laden slopes that dropped sharply to meet the water. That night, I slept on the ground with my face pointed toward my village and the ocean front I would never have the joy of seeing again.

"You know, he delivered me to Julio in Veracruz and didn't even stay the night, but returned that same day. Perhaps he felt he might weaken if he stayed any longer. 'Don't worry, Primo,' I remember Julio saying to my father, 'I'll instruct him well.' And with those words my father left. I never returned home nor saw him or my mother again.

"Julio was a brute, cunning and cruel, a braggart and drunkard who didn't hesitate to belittle me or give me a hard, quick slap when he thought I wasn't being alert. He put me to work immediately, the same day my father left me. 'Here you work,' he said, giving me over to the hard-looking man who managed his hired labor. I had to prove that I was no idiot before Julio even took notice of me. After a few weeks, he began to give me orders directly, allowing me to run some short errands for him. His house was dark and smelled closed off, as if the man didn't want any air to get in or out. He shut himself off from anything fresh or fragrant. He gave me a small room on the other side of the house, but it wasn't far enough that I couldn't hear him snoring and farting all night. It made me sad to hear him, that gassy son-of-a-bitch. Puro pedo ese cabrón. I soon learned that no one liked him. His workers, who knew him best because they experienced his brutality firsthand, called him el chango because he was small but alert. His features were pointed, however, and to me he looked more like a ratón.

"It wasn't often that I got to walk the bright, complicated streets of Veracruz, but when he let me out alone, I would head for the docks. In those days they were filled with cargo ships coming from nations I knew nothing of—France, Germany, Argentina—places I imagined visiting one day. In those days there were men there who still remembered the war against the French. Many had visited foreign countries and would tell you a story if you were polite and said nothing. In my imaginings the cities of those countries always looked something like my village. Veracruz had not yet been overrun by turistas, gawking gringos who know nothing but how to take pictures. When sent off to run an errand, I would take a circuitous route. To me, the Castle of San Juan de Ulúa promised a hiding place. At least it did at first. I was a child, you see, five or six years younger than you are. I imagined then that there were places to hide. The castle, with its turrets outlined against gray, stormy skies, seemed solitary and invincible, a place where I might run to escape Julio. But as the years passed, I realized the castle was not a refuge, but the image of what I must become in order to withstand the pain of life.

"One day, it was during the dog days, in July or August, I do not remember very well anymore, my cousin sent me to buy him liquor. I went feeling good. It was very hot, however, hotter than it is outside this box, almost as hot as it will get tomorrow. But I was excited. I decided to run to town to have spare time for myself. I got there sweaty, panting. I first went to the liquor store and bought my cousin his bottle.

"I made my way outside and began to walk around. I wanted to see the red-domed Church of Santo Cristo. Julio didn't go to mass, and I missed the strength and certainty such ritual brings. I looked for the cathedral, its white campanario beckoning believers to prayer. I didn't go to kneel. I'd given up on that hopeful gesture. But I did like the idea of faith, that somehow the campanario pointed us in the right direction. Childish romanticism, always turning toward the light of the sky. Few people were walking the streets. I tell you it was well over a hundred degrees. I gave up the idea of walking to the church. As I passed the few stores, most of them closed until the evening, I looked in the windows at the trinkets, boots, saddles, and belts.

"I wanted a caballo, one on which I would be able to ride fast, fast enough to get away from the heat. I had a secret thought. I would ride to my cousin's house and say: 'Julio, come out here now. We must talk.'

"He would be furious that I had dared to call for him. He would storm out with hate on his little face, all eyebrows, thinking only of the cuff he was going to deliver me. But then he would see me on the horse, and for a moment he would be even more furious, thinking that I had stolen the horse, or that it was one of his. I would then say: 'Do not worry, Julio, the horse is not yours; it is mine, Julio, all mine. Tú no me lo distes.'

"Then his face would darken and explode in fury. He would be ready to kill me with his bare hands. I would see the murder in his eyes, and I would laugh loudly, bravely in his face. 'I came only to tell you I'm leaving now. I've decided to go to Chihuahua, where I will be a caballero.'

"Then he would shriek like a woman, 'You'll go nowhere, you horse thief. They'll hang you, cabrón!' and on and on and on.

"I would only smile, spurring my horse gently, turning him around while my cousin screamed until his throat bled. I would ride away, slowly at first. Then when his ravings had been swallowed by the wind, I would spur the horse and ride at full gallop until I got to Chihuahua.

"That's why I loved to look in the shops at the saddles and boots. I had a paper on which I calculated the prices of the leather. It was my dream, you see. And so I was walking that day in Veracruz, looking at my dreams through the windows, when an old woman called out to me. 'Hijo,' she said, 'help me to my room, por favor.'

"She was a cripple. She sat in a wheelchair, one of her legs missing. She was carrying a box filled with provisions. 'Help me, please,' she pleaded. I could see the sweat on her face. She had gone out at the wrong time, like me. As I pushed her along she talked about the heat and how it was insufferable. The sun was pouring fire, it seemed. She kept chattering, motioning with her hand when we came to a street she wanted me to turn down. 'Aquí' she would say, before continuing her prattle. And then it happened." Berto's faced grimaced. "The bottle of tequila fell from beneath my arm. 'Ahh,' was all I could manage to think before the awful sound of shattering glass. The old woman didn't even notice. She kept talking and talking. My stomach began to turn. I knew what my cousin would do. He would accuse me of spending the money on something else, drinks or a whore, anything not to believe me. I began to panic. I knew he would beat me, but more than that, I hated what that beating would mean. Beatings made me feel helpless, his control over me established with every blow.

"As I thought about my bad luck, the old woman directed me to her house. Left, she would say, right, and all the time the sun driving me down, beating me down, the heat boiling my insides. I felt like a frog that bursts in the sun.

"I began to resent the old woman and her torn leg. I felt an intense hatred of her. She, old and withered, oblivious to anything but her desire to get home and her luck at encountering a stupid child who would push her home. I cursed her in my mind. I thought she should pay for what she was doing, for what she had done. Sweat poured from my face; down my hands it poured, and I looked at them, my hands, and they trembled as I gripped the handles of the old woman's wheelchair. At that moment I decided I must kill her for what she had done. I saw myself gripping her by the throat. Her surprise as her eyes bugged out. Her wanting with all her might to scream, but my hands would be wrapped around her little sagging throat so tight that no breath could escape.

"But we were still in plain sight, so I began to look for a hidden place where I might kill her unnoticed. 'Here,' she said. We had arrived at her house. I thought, why not kill her in her own home and then steal her money to buy tequila for Julio? I would squeeze the old woman's bones, pouring her life into Julio's glass that night.

"I pushed her into her house. 'Let me get you something to drink,' she said. I nodded. I wanted to spring at her and drag her off the chair, but I froze and she left the room. That moment was like a knife that wanted to cut me, slice me, bleed me. I ran. I ran in that heat all the way home. Julio almost broke my arm that night. But I won, because it was the heat that had tried to beat me, and it had not done so. Even my fear of Julio had not been strong enough to make me act out my darkest impulse."

Berto laughed. "I didn't want to scare you, but you asked me if the heat had ever made me crazy."

"You think that'll happen in here?" I asked.

"I don't know, boy. Perhaps it has already begun to happen."

By this time, the water in the barrel was almost gone. Only a gallon or two remained, and we had not yet been on the train a complete day.

Night overtook us. The heat was still uncomfortable, probably in the nineties, but it was blessed relief from the afternoon's misery. The box again became dark as the night threw a blanket over the few cracks that let light through during the day. Berto fell asleep. It was his snore that had reminded me of my father. I closed my eyes and tried to fall asleep. I prayed for my mother and for the Virgin to keep me and her safe.

*    *    *

I woke up thinking I was in my room, but soon I fell back to sleep. I didn't want to dream of anything bad so I thought of my father, hoping he might speak to me as I slept. It worked. I saw him there in the darkness, floating before me.

I smiled at him and he stood there nodding back. I said hello to him, but he didn't say anything. I repeated my greeting louder. "Hello, Papi," I yelled. But still he said nothing. I began to cry, pleading with my father to say something. Instead he disappeared and I saw only the blackness again. Then I heard his voice. I could not understand his words; they sounded muffled. I was alone, in my bed, my mouth pressed against a rough blanket. I stifled my cries of anguish with the coarse wool. No one came, but still I heard the muffled voice of my father coming from an unseen room. I waited in dread, wanting with all my heart for someone to come to me. Fear covered me, horror froze me. The reason for my fear was not known to me. I cried because of the darkness in my room, because it was fighting me, laughing at me. Tears ran down my face as I waited for him. But instead my mother came and tried to comfort me. She stroked my hair, and the warmth of her hand gradually calmed me. Then she sang, slowly ushering me into sleep. She watched, singing softer and softer, until my eyes grew heavy and closed. Then she left, and the part of me that never sleeps knew I was alone again. The fear my mother had driven away returned. Now it was stronger, no longer laughing but screaming as it taunted me. I cried louder. This time my father came, but he was angry and had a belt in his hand, and he hit me and left. I am now awake, I thought, and then everything was drowned out by the darkness, but he came into the room several times to hit me because I would not stop crying.

Then the darkness became constant, and my father beating me became the pulse of the darkness, the rhythm of my fear.

I woke up, opening my eyes and seeing only the darkness of the box. I was afraid, and I touched Berto's arm.

"Are you awake?" I asked.

"Yes, Luis, what's the matter?"

"Nothing, I just wanted to check."

"You were having a bad dream," he said.

"Yes. But it's already fading," I lied.

"Oh."

"Berto," I said, "I woke you because I was scared. Scared of the darkness. Just silliness," I said, feeling ashamed now.

"I don't blame you for being scared of the dark, Luis. I too have never liked the dark. Many men are afraid to face the night. The cantinas are filled with old and young, all together. They congregate to escape having to be alone in the night, where the reality of separation makes itself felt." He patted my shoulder. "There is no shame in fearing that," he said, settling back to fall asleep.

"Why do you think these men have left?"

"Why have you left?" he asked me.

"I can't explain it. I had to come, to see what truth lay in all those stories I've heard about el norte. Besides, there's no way to help my mother in Bustamante. Everything seems dead to me there. Everyone walks the same street every day, doing the same things, seeing the same people, giving each other the same greeting. When I left, I felt like a great explorer, going to see things others didn't dare to see."

"It was a great risk, boy."

"You took it also."

"I had no choice in the matter. Choice belongs only to the young, the rich, and the fool. Let me sleep, Luis," he said, turning away from me.

I lay awake all that night. My hands explored the floor. It was coarse wood, splintered. Pain shot through my hand, and I drew it to my mouth. I had a sliver of wood in my palm. I pulled it out. It was over an inch long.

The metallic taste of blood filled my mouth. I heard moaning. A man spoke softly, comfortingly. "We'll be there soon. Then things will be better. Believe me."

*   *   *

"You idiots. We're going to die in here. Let's use the axe to break the doors. I'll be damned if I die in a railcar with you pigs!" It was Chico.

"Shut up," Berto said. "If you don't shut up the rest of us will have to kill you. Rosales told us what it would be like and we all agreed. Now shut up or I'll rip your tongue out myself."

The old man stood before Chico, glaring at him. For a moment no one moved. They all stared at the old man. Chico finally looked away, settling back against the wall.

"We'll all die in here. Pendejos." He spit against the wall, then looked down at his feet.

The water was now gone. Berto had been right. Some of the men were now urinating in the barrel.

We had no idea if we were close to Texas. All through the box men were trying to decide whether or not we were across the border. Some even figured we were only miles from the Valley. Rosales had said we would be there within thirty-six hours, but we were already well into the second day.

The boxcar smelled of urine and shit. I myself had to defecate behind the bale of hay. The heat of midday was only a couple of hours away, and then I knew the smell would become unbearable.

I was beginning to get hungry. I had already eaten the nuts and dried fruit I'd brought. I knew that I would soon be delirious with thirst and that I could not drink the water in my canteen unnoticed. I told Berto of my hidden water.

"Save it," he said. "Save it for when the heat has sweated the very last out of you. You'll need it most then. Then you won't care if any of the men are willing to kill you for it. You'll be ready to kill too."

Chico was mumbling now. He felt foolish. He knew that Berto had made him look like a coward. No one listened to him as he sat alone cursing us all.

The heat was overpowering. I had learned to judge the time of day by the temperature in the box. At its hottest I knew it was near three; at its coolest, it was the middle of the night. By the way the men were beginning to sweat and were drowsing off, I knew it was around noon. The real heat would start in the next couple of hours.

# Chapter Five

The train had stopped again, and the heat pressed against us. One of the men had become delirious. He moaned quietly at first, and only every so often. He did not have any friends. After about an hour he began to moan a name, a woman's name. It sounded like "María." I am not sure whether he meant the Virgin or his wife.

Still the train did not move, but soon we heard men talking outside the boxcar. They talked in Spanish. We were still in Mexico. The men outside were discussing how long it would be before the train started on its way. The delirious man started to moan again, loudly now.

"Shut him up," said Alejandro. "If they hear him they'll open up this box. Remember what Rosales said."

No one moved. The man began to cry softly. "María," he said, "María, ¡ayúdame!" he cried. "Alejandro," said Pablo, "shut him up or I'll use the axe."

Alejandro went over to the man. "Shut your mouth or we'll be discovered. Be quiet." He slapped the man hard.

None of us moved. I watched as the sick man put his hands over his mouth. "It hurts," he moaned. He stifled a cry, like a child, sniffling loudly. "María!" he cried again. "María, ¿dónde estás?"

This time Alejandro took a rag from his pocket. He violently shoved his hands over the man's face. The man began to kick wildly with both legs.

"Help me, idiots," hissed Alejandro.

The Guatemalan grabbed the man's legs and sat on them. Still the man struggled, his wild screams muted by Alejandro's hands. He was suffocating. For a moment I was sure Alejandro would kill him like that. But then the man stuck his finger into Alejandro's eye. Alejandro did not scream. He fell back clutching his face with both hands. He rolled onto his stomach, shaking his head in pain.

The Guatemalan struck the man in the mouth. But the man was now wild. I didn't see Pablo pick up the axe. I was watching the Guatemalan struggle with the delirious man.

"Let's see," said Pablo.

The Guatemalan looked up and moved back quickly. I do not think the man saw the axe coming. Pablo struck him through the top of the head. Blood sprayed through the air, reaching even me, though I was several feet away. The man did not even moan. His legs stopped kicking, his body in shock. His arms were thrown back as if he had fallen suddenly from a chair. His hands quivered for a few moments and then stopped.

No one said anything. The boxcar was completely quiet as Pablo pulled the axe from the man's skull. He walked back to the bale of hay and threw the axe on it casually, then sat down. Alejandro was now sitting up. He was still clutching his eye, blood seeping through his fingers.

"Clean your face," Berto said to me.

I wiped the man's blood from my face.

"Your story about the heat," I said. "Did you know?"

"I hoped not, but I knew there was the chance with so many men and so little water. Everyone trapped in here has desperate motives. I've seen enough men to know that something of this sort could happen under these circumstances. Perhaps you knew as well. The heat makes one crazy."

"I'd never go that crazy," I whispered to him.

"Maybe it's the strongest who must make such choices for us. Would you rather the men outside had heard and come in here?"

I said nothing.

"I know. You think the men out there knew we were in here the whole time, right? Maybe they did; maybe they didn't care. Maybe Rosales paid them off. Perhaps there weren't even any men out there. But what about when we're in Texas, and the men out there aren't bribed federales or drunken railmen? What about when there are four or five delirious men in here, all moaning for their mothers, praying for the Virgin to rescue them. Rosales told us. He told us it would be rough. What about when some of these idiots are so crazed with thirst that they're willing to drink the hot piss out of that barrel? What then?"

"He didn't have to kill him," I said.

"In any war there must be death. This is a struggle now," he said quietly. "Perhaps more will die. The only thing to be done now is to make sure you survive, and the only way to do so is to harden yourself. You can't be concerned about the others or you'll die with them. It's not pretty to think this way, but it's necessary on a journey that has turned brutal."

\*　　\*　　\*

Several hours had passed since the sick man had been killed. No one had moved the body, although two or three men had complained that in the heat the body would soon begin to rot. Alejandro was still nursing his eye. "Cabrón. Crazy man," he muttered every few minutes.

Pablo sat alone. He had said nothing since the murder. The axe still lay on the bale, the blood now dried.

"No one is saying anything. It's as if nothing happened," I said.

"What is there to say?" said Berto. "These men have seen worse. They've lived through worse. I myself saw my own daughter die. I had to bury her alone. Do you understand? What is one fool's death when set against that?"

"Nothing," I agreed.

"What do I care about the death of a fool?" he said harshly, as if banishing the thought from his own stubborn mind. He looked toward the corpse. "He had a choice. Others do not."

"Who doesn't have a choice?" I asked.

"A little girl," he said, reclining against the wall. "Children have no choice. Things happen to them, horrible things, disease, beatings, starvation. They don't even have the words to tell."

"What happened?"

"My wife and I had a child soon after we married. We had a girl, a healthy girl. We named her Celia, for the heavens. She was beautiful. Long black hair and dark eyes like her mother's. But she was stubborn like me. I could tell as soon as she was born that she would be strong. We would put her in her highchair, my wife would feed her, and then she would serve me my dinner. Once we ignored her for too long while we were eating. Suddenly my wife gasped.

" 'Berto,' she cried, 'the baby!' I turned to look. Celia's face was puffed up like a bullfrog and red as a tomato. I thought she was choking. But no. She was impatient with sitting in the chair, and instead of crying out she had puffed up. I knew then my Celia would be strong, not a crier.

"I taught her to walk. I gave her her baths. I gave her rides on my shoulders. I heard her first words. And even though I myself have never been very religious, I knew I must have her baptized by the Church, to have her dedicated. But we did not have the time." He stopped talking.

"How did she die?" I asked.

He sat until the weight of the silence forced me to speak. "Finish the story."

He turned toward me and said, "Later. Anyway, you're not my confessor. I'll have to wait to find a priest to make my peace with God. But I'll tell you this. I went to Chihuahua much later. I found that life was the same there, the same as it was in Oaxaca, the same as in Veracruz, the same as in this fucking box. Back then I thought only one thing mattered. Foolishly I believed that if I did that one thing, then all I had suffered would be bearable. This path, misguided and lonely, has led me here."

*    *    *

The train began to move again, but the heat was still very bad for us all. The dead man was beginning to smell. I did not want to look at him but I did anyway. It was growing dark, and all I could make out was a shape. He was very still, which proved to me that he was indeed dead. When the train started up again, the body rolled forward, not naturally, but like a log. I imagined what it would be like to touch it. I had felt a dead body before. It was my father's. I was very sad when he died although I did not understand until later the depth of my sadness. When he was laid out in a box in the church, I did not want to see him. From where I sat I could just make out his nose. It didn't look like his nose, and although I didn't want to see him, my eyes were drawn toward that unnaturally gray lump. It looked like clay, like wet clay that my grandmother had just shaped.

When the priest finished the mass, all the people lined up to see my father's body. They all cried and said goodbye. My mother walked to the casket. My uncle held her and she wept loudly, as if she would never stop.

"Go to your mother," my aunt urged me. "Comfort her. You're the man now. Go, it's your place now."

But I didn't want to go to her. I felt strange, as if I were merely a witness, as if I were there to watch, not to get involved.

My aunt prodded me from behind. "Go, Luis."

So I got up slowly and walked to the front of the church. My mother was still weeping in front of the casket. My uncle was holding her up, trying to steady her, but her sobs shook her so violently that even he seemed unsteady, almost as if he were dizzy. I stood behind my mother and looked into the casket. My father was not there. No one was there. But maybe if you touch it, I thought, you'll see that it's real.

"Your father, mijo, your father," my mother sobbed.

I reached into the casket with my finger and drew it across his forehead. It did not seem real. It was cold, and his skin felt hard, like a cool rock. I closed my eyes and imagined I was touching a table, and I could not tell the difference.

When they buried him, I was glad it was over. Not till later, days later, did his death become real to me. It was getting cold and there was no firewood. I went to get the axe, but it wasn't there. So as I had done hundreds of times before, I started to turn back to the house to ask my father for it. Then I remembered. I would have to find the axe on my own. I would have to find everything on my own. I must now be my own father.

*    *    *

"Why did you come here, Berto?"

"To get away, just like everyone else in this box."

"But what are you getting away from?"

"El diablo."

"I don't believe in the devil."

"That means nothing. You've never seen him and I have."

"If you've seen the devil, what does he look like? Does he have horns and chicken feet?"

"No, he doesn't look at all like that. He can look like anything. The first time I saw him was a few months ago. He came to me as darkness. You think I'm crazy, but I've spent half my life in darkness, and I know what it feels like. This was different, muy diferente. It was quiet, but the quiet was loud and empty. My eyes were completely open, but I couldn't see anything at all, not even shadows. And then I couldn't move. I wanted to get up but I couldn't. This is what it's like to be dead, I thought. I struggled within myself to move, but still I lay there, my eyes wide open.

" 'You're here, aren't you?' I said.

" 'Estoy aquí.' It was only a whisper. Only a whisper.

" 'I'm here and I've got hold of you, viejo.' I lay there until morning, looking up into the darkness all night. The devil surrounded me, holding me, not letting me move until the light sent him away. But he returned with the darkness night after night. I feel him now.

"That is how I understand your fear of the darkness, Luis. That dead one saw him also. He saw him just as I saw him that night. The only difference was that Pablo was not there to end it for me."

Berto put his hand on my knee.

"I'm old, and I'll die soon, but it won't be in a dark room, alone, not being able to move while the devil plays with me. I know he has followed me. He'll have to keep following me, too. I don't intend to wait for him helplessly. The fucker has had to search. He's on this train now, but now at least there'll be witnesses. You'll be a witness."

"You're talking nonsense," I said. "We're going to America. There's no devil there. They'd stop him at the border. Do you think the federales would let him through? No, he has much too much to do here to waste his time following an old man to America."

"No," said Berto, "he is here."

*   *   *

The body had begun to rot.

"Let's put the hay over him," said Chico.

"Yes, that's what we have to do," said another man.

Alejandro looked at Pablo. Pablo still sat in the same place against the wall. He had not said anything since the killing. He had retrieved the axe and laid it across his lap. No one moved toward the bale. All eyes turned toward Pablo.

"Leave him there," he said.

"Fuck that, Pablo," said Chico. "He'll make us all sick. By tomorrow the stench will have us all vomiting. We've got to at least cover him."

"You won't do anything, Chico, except what I tell you."

"We're not going to get sick. We have to cover him." Chico looked at us, but no one said anything.

"We'll all be sick by tomorrow," he muttered. "You'll all see. A dead man decaying here on the floor, and we don't have the sense to cover him with hay." Chico sat down, covering his face with his shirt.

"You still don't believe in el diablo?" Berto whispered next to me.

# Chapter Six

It was night again. My prayers had done no good. The only thing I had to be thankful for was that the train was moving again. My thirst had become so unbearable that I decided to drink from my canteen. I took it from my bedroll quietly and unscrewed the cap very slowly. I was scared that someone might be awake, so I waited almost an hour to drink from it. I only took one drink. I shook Berto. He woke quietly, but when I offered him the canteen he refused.

"Later, when I need it more," he said. I carefully put the canteen back in my bedroll. I felt guilty because the other men in the box were suffering, but I knew they would fight over it, and I remembered Pablo's axe.

"Why won't he let us put hay over the body?" I whispered.

"It wouldn't matter anyway. Do you think for a minute that a few stalks of hay could keep that stench from filling every meter of this box? It doesn't matter. The rot will not be covered by hay."

"I think he's crazy anyway," I said.

"He's crazy, but he's not a lunatic," Berto said. "He knows the hay won't protect the air, but he does it to prove that he's in charge here. He is el jefe."

"What if he begins to kill others?"

"What does it matter? We're all dead; it's just taking us longer to start rotting. I feel it happening to me already. I told you the devil would follow me." He stared at Pablo.

"Look," he said, "he has found me now, even here. Like my old grandmother used to tell me, he knows no borders. But this time I'm not alone. It would have been better for me to stay on my farm. Now that he's found me with so many men, he'll take us all." He managed a snicker. "It's a good day for him when he can get extra souls when he came for only one."

"Berto," I said, "he's only a man." I looked at Pablo. "What makes him think we won't take the axe from him?"

"These men are all weak with thirst and hunger. We'll all be sick soon."

The night passed slowly, but the train's movement rocked me to sleep. When I awoke it was still dark and cool in the boxcar, but we had stopped again. All I heard was the quiet snores and heavy breathing of the men. My stomach was churning. I put my shirt over my face and tried to think of something else, of getting to Texas. I hoped we were already there. But it did no good. I crawled to an empty corner and vomited. Nothing came up except for a little spit. I stayed there heaving for some time. When I finally stopped, I felt very weak. I tried to stand, but I fell backward. I could not tell whether the train was moving or whether I was still falling. It was as if I were suspended from a rope being swung though the pitch dark. I enjoyed the feeling for a few moments, weightless, my senses confused, no longer transmitting my pain. I felt only lightness. But as soon as the sensation had started, I came to myself as my back hit the wood floor. I tried to stand but could not find the strength even to crawl back to where I'd been sitting. Instead, I sat back against the wall where I had landed. I did not want to lie down again because my stomach still felt very bad. I wondered if I was dying and if I would die. I wondered what dying would feel like. I remembered watching my father die long ago. I could not bring back very much. I remembered only that one moment he had been putting tar on our roof and the next he was on the ground, twisted and moaning.

My mother had run out of the house screaming. I remember those shrieks. She couldn't stop. Even as I ran to get help, I could hear her. He was a strong man. He tried hard to live, but he had broken his neck, the doctor said, and even breathing was too much of a task. "There's nothing to do now," he told us. My father lay on his bed, unconscious, but I sat there knowing that as long as his chest heaved, he was still there. "He doesn't feel anything," the doctor assured me privately as my mother sat in another room with our neighbors. "He'll go quickly, painlessly. It's almost better this way." I sat there feeling as if I was only watching. "You're going to have to be the man for your mother, boy. If he were to live, he'd be in this bed the rest of his life. I've known him since he was your age, and he wouldn't want that." With those words, he left to tend to my mother. I sat there listening to his breathing, feeling guilty that I wanted him to live, even if it was only for the sound of his breath.

And then he was dead.

Now his body rotted in the ground back in Bustamante. Rotting, as would my body in the darkness of this box. The stench seemed to get stronger, and I tried to stop breathing because I knew I was taking in death.

"Luis," I heard Berto call. "Luis, where are you?"

"I'm here," I said. I slowly crawled back to him.

"He's here again," he said.

"Who? Who's here, Berto?"

"The devil. He's finally come to claim me. I saw him just a moment ago," Berto whispered.

"No, no, Berto. It's only a bad dream. I've been awake. I was watching. I could hear you snoring. It was only a dream."

"You don't understand. You can't see him. He's not here for you. He's here for me. He's torturing me. I'm the only one that sees him. Es mi culpa. Don't you understand? It's my punishment. It's been my punishment from the beginning."

"You're talking crazy, Berto. Why would the devil be here for you? You haven't done anything to him or for him. You're a simple man who's led a simple life. You've done nothing but suffer. Think—why would the devil, or God, or anybody want to punish you?"

He lifted his destroyed hand and stroked my cheek. "This is the mark I carry to remind me of my sin, and this is the mark by which the devil knows me."

"What sin?" I asked. "What are you talking about? I don't understand you, Berto. I tell you, you're just scared. I am too. We have to be in Texas already. Understand? We'll be out of here soon."

"No, Luis. We'll never get out of here. This is my purgatory. My sin is being purged. Maybe then God will accept me, but first the devil must have his turn. Don't you see? I have to pay."

"Why? What for?" I asked.

"No," he said quietly, exhausted from our conversation.

"What did you do?" I asked him impatiently.

"Yes, I must tell you." His voice cracked with grief. "I told you before that I came so that I would have a witness. Someone must bear witness to my sin, to my sentence, and to my torment. There is no priest here. I may not live to find a priest. You will hear my confession.

"I have sown all that's befallen me. Many times I have wished I was dead. But instead it has fallen to me to watch those I love suffer for my transgressions—my daughter and my wife."

Berto paused. He seemed to be preparing, setting events and details straight in his mind. I waited to hear the confession of a blasphemer, of one irretrievably lost. I did not want to hear it.

"I remember the day I left my cousin. It's still very clear in my mind. I think you should remember well the beginning of your ruination. At least I have that, no? I can still remember it all.

"I had been with Julio seven years, and I was now about the same age as you, boy. For those long years of hard work I had been rewarded with more beatings than I could count. He kept a close watch on me. He was suspicious, perhaps that I would run away or that I was stealing from him. He rarely let me go into town alone unless he was too drunk to go or too hung over, and then he would send me. Even though such trips usually ended with a tirade of accusations or worse, I looked forward to them for the temporary freedom they gave me.

"Didn't you write to your mother and father? Couldn't you have gone back home?"

"No. After my father left me, Julio let me know that my father had turned over to him all parental authority. 'I have it written on paper. You are apprenticed to me. But you are much more than that, boy. You are quite legally my "son." You won't be going back so you'd better get used to me and Veracruz. I'm your papá here. My word is final and I won't have it questioned. If you do what you're told and are a quick learner and hard worker, life here won't be too bad. You'll learn what took me years of hard experience to learn.'

"He was cruel, but I must admit I learned as much from him as I did from my true father. I suppose that makes him my real father then, no?"

"How did you finally manage to escape?"

"Escape? I don't think such a thing exists. It's more accurate to ask how I managed to leave. It's possible to do that, but escape?"

"Then how did you leave?"

"I had dreamt of that day so often, but when it came, it happened as suddenly and unexpectedly as a brushfire overtaking a farmer lost in a daydream. We took a wagon that morning because we were going to pick up some cotton cloth that my cousin had been anxiously awaiting. Coarse cottons sold fast in the summer, and he expected to make many pesos.

"He told me he was going to be rich and that I should be grateful for his help. 'Do you hate me because I'm hard on you, Berto?' he asked. I'd heard that question too many times. It was a warning to me to be circumspect. With Julio, such a question was thorny. I could not tell him the truth, that I loathed him and that I regularly fantasized about his murder. Nor could I tell him I appreciated his patronage without giving lie to such a statement. I tried to sound sincere but unemotional. 'No, Cousin. I understand the help you are giving me.'

" 'I'm glad you appreciate it, Berto. You must understand that I'm making you a man. In the seven years you've been with me, I've seen you grow from a child into a joven that your father would be satisfied with. You know, I plan to have many men working under me, and when you have many men working for you, you must watch them. Men steal when they have no one watching them. They're lazy and need discipline. Discipline starts with fear, and not fear of being dismissed. No, it must be a deeper fear. It must be a fear that cuts so deep into their souls that it keeps them from doing what they ought not do.

" '¿Comprendes? This is a fear of the mind, not a fear rooted in reality. This fear is irrational. It feeds on the mind, growing larger and larger until it is so large that a man is paralyzed and afraid to act on his own. That man will do anything you ask. When a man is finally under control, you no longer have to watch him so closely.

" 'To inspire such fear is the essence of a real leader, a man who is a success. I am that kind of man, Berto.' He looked at me and smiled.

" 'Of course, you don't possess this quality yet. You're honest and hardworking, I'll give you that much, but you're too soft here,' he said, thumping his chest. 'You have a long, hard journey ahead of you if you can't control your actions with your head and not your heart. You leave that to your woman. If you ever get one, you'll find out why they can't lead or even think. They'll exasperate you. You must harden yourself or your time will be filled with pain and suffering.

Perhaps that's what you need. A bit of suffering. In the end you'll come out of it like me. You must die to yourself and be reborn as a hard, rational man. That is what marks one as a success.'

"We came to the warehouse where the cotton was. We loaded it, but there were many bundles and it took the better part of the morning. When we finished we were both tired and thirsty.

" '¿Una cerveza?' my cousin asked as if he were offering me my freedom. He tried to smile. 'You've worked hard.'

"We went to a cantina and drank beer. He drank heavily, as he always did when he had reason to be satisfied. He drank alone when he was miserable, but the cotton had made him almost giddy. After I finished my beer, he told me to go out and mind the wagon. I sat out there for an hour, and still Julio did not come out. I peeped in and saw him talking to two men I didn't know, probably townsmen who had been lured into conversation for the price of a round of cheap tequila. It was his favorite ploy. I can tell you not many men drank with him twice. Aside from being a braggart and a bore, his drinking usually ended in insults and sometimes blows. He didn't take kindly to anyone leaving in the middle of one of his stories, either. But the bastard was boring, and you can't blame someone for wanting to get away from a man who goes on about his power to exploit and make money. Often he'd come home with a black eye or split lip, cursing, always cursing, and looking for me to take the brunt of his petty revenge.

"Anyway, seeing him in such company, I decided I had some time. Just around the block from the cantina was a saddle shop, so I stole away to go look. Not for very long. I just wanted to see them. I didn't believe Julio's claims that he'd be rich one day, or that he could transform me into a lying, vicious cabrón such as he was, no matter how many times he beat me or cajoled me. But I knew that my father would die, and then I would get my pay. You see, as an apprentice I was not entitled to anything but room and board, but Julio had agreed to pay my father a small yearly sum for my labor. At my majority, I would be entitled to wages. Then I would get a horse and saddle.

"I made my way to the saddle shop. I had been there many times and the owner knew me by name.

" 'You going to buy a saddle today, Berto?' asked the owner. He always asked the same question and I always responded, 'I think I have to buy a horse first.'

" 'Yes, I see your problem. Well, as often as you come in here, God must have noticed by now, eh?'

" 'Perhaps he will,' I said." Berto stared into the darkness of the boxcar, lost in the saddle shop he was describing.

"Berto," I said. I shook him gently.

"God did not hear me," he said so softly that I almost lost the words.

"Tell me what happened then, Berto."

"The wagon was gone. I thought someone had stolen the cotton. I ran into the bar to tell Julio, but he was also gone. The bartender told me he had left with a bottle of tequila.

"I was relieved, but I knew that Julio would beat me with as much vigor as if the cotton had been stolen. With the same vigor as he would have beaten me had I given the cotton away.

"I waited until it was dark, hoping that Julio would drink himself into a stupor. It was a tactic I had learned soon after I arrived.

"That night I walked into the house from the back, entering through the kitchen. Julio was sitting at the table with a lantern set low. He was still drinking.

" 'Well, cabroncito, you finally decided to come home, eh?' I stood there looking at my shoes. 'I spend all day telling you that I want you to be my partner, the supervisor of my workers. I tell you that you must be responsible, that you must be rigid . . .'

"He waited for me to say something to try to excuse myself, but I said nothing.

" 'I give you a simple instruction: Go sit in the wagon. Take care of my goods, take care of my future, my profit, and when I come out, what do I see? My wagon and my cloth but no Berto. You'd run off to play like a child.'

"He poured himself another glass of tequila. 'But I should have known you weren't ready yet, even though I've spent so much time trying to show you what it takes to be a man. Remember I told you it would take a long, painful journey for you to become worthy? You even thanked me for it. I have to be vigilant with you, like a father. Who is more your father than I? Not that man who sent you here.' He waited for me to respond, but I stayed quiet, not sure of what he wanted to hear and feeling ashamed that I had left the cotton.

" 'You don't answer me!' His voice began to rise in anger. 'You think anyone cares for you like me? Not your parents, if that's what you hope for when you lie in your room. Your father, he told me when he left you here that I could do with you as I pleased. I could have made you sleep in the barn or on the floor of the warehouse like some of the workers. But instead I took you in and gave you a place in my own house. I have treated you like familia. No, like my own son. And for my fatherly concern you pay me back with insolence. No, worse. With complete contempt.'

"Julio stood slowly. He was not very steady, and his hands were trembling. I could tell he was very drunk.

" 'I'll make you worthy. I've made it a goal. You think I'll allow you to prove me a failure? I've promised you would become a man, a hard man. Like me.' He pointed at himself.

"Then the devil entered me," Berto said. "I looked at my cousin and whispered, 'I don't want to be like you.'

"Julio began walking toward me. He had a thick cane in his hand. I began moving backward.

" 'I don't want to be like you,' I said again, but this time loudly and to his face.

"He hit me on the face with the cane. The blow caught me on the cheek, and I fell back. I had not expected him to be so quick.

" 'You little bastard,' he cursed, preparing to hit me again. 'You have no father, but you have a master, and I'll be damned if you won't know it after I finish with you. After tonight your own flesh and bone will testify to that.'

"He swung at me again, but this time I moved out of the way. My cheek was bleeding and already swollen. I brushed my hand across it and felt the blood and felt the pain shooting through my face. I began to cry. At the sight of my tears, my cousin began to taunt me.

" 'You cry like a baby. No, worse . . . a woman.' And he swung at me again. Now I was backed against the wall. The cane hit my shoulder. The pain was enough to send me to the floor. I covered my head as Julio struck my hands and shoulders over and over.

" 'You're going to be strong, strong like me. Strong. Strong. Strong!' he yelled.

"I tried to make a fist to hit him with, but I could not bend my fingers. I could not even lift my hand. I could feel that my right shoulder was broken. Julio was still pelting me with the cane. I realized he would break my head if I didn't stop him. With my left hand I grabbed his hip, and I pulled him forward as I struck him in the groin with my head. Julio bent over, dropping his cane, which I grabbed. He looked at me. For the first time I saw astonishment on his face. That cabrón! It was like his dick had been ripped away and he was about to be whipped with it, and by a goddamn child! He couldn't believe that I had dared hit him or that I held his precious cane.

" 'Give me that cane,' he said. He was still bent over, holding his huevos with both his hands.

"I got up, but instead of giving him the cane, I hit him over the back with it. He cursed at me. I'm not sure what he said. I began to hit him furiously. He fell on his face, covering his head with his hands, just as I had.

" 'You bastard, you and my father!' I said. 'Bastard,' I screamed as I beat him with the cane. I hit him on the buttocks and legs over and over, until Julio stopped thrashing around and just lay there moaning. I backed off from him.

" 'Why would I want to be like you?' I said, crying.

"I took the cane and swung it at the bottle standing on the table. It crashed, sending broken glass all over the floor. It was a release for me. I stopped thinking and started breaking everything I could with the cane. I broke the windows and the glasses. Then I ran into the room in which he did his accounting. I threw his desk over and smashed his chair against the wall.

" 'Cabrón,' I heard my cousin moaning from the kitchen. 'I'll kill you for this, you'll see.'

"I walked back to the kitchen. He was trying to stand, but his legs were in pain and very unsteady.

" 'You'll pay!' he yelled.

"I wanted to kill him. ¿Entiendes? And I was going to kill him, but then it occurred to me that there was another way. I took his lantern and walked outside. I walked to the barn, which Julio was using that night to store the cotton he'd been too drunk to take to his warehouse. I went in, leaving the door open behind me. I walked over to the wagon, which had not been unloaded. Julio had been so drunk that he had not even bothered to unharness the horses. I slowly took the bit from their mouths and the heavy harnesses from their backs.

"My right shoulder was useless. I heard Julio come walking out into the yard. He was yelling that he was going to shoot me. I saddled one of the horses as quickly as I could. Julio was getting closer. His voice boomed.

" 'I'm going to teach you. I'm going to teach you what a man does to demand respect!' he yelled, coming closer.

"I jumped on the horse, and with my good arm I threw the lantern onto the wagon. It burst into flame, the cotton giving off a bright gold light. My cousin's profit burned very beautifully.

"Julio let out a howl when he heard the fire. As I spurred the horse out of the barn, he ran toward me with his gun pointed. He shot at me, but as unsteady as the tequila and beating had made his aim, he missed. I galloped away, not hearing the thundering of the horse's hooves, conscious only of the wind's scream and the eerie glow of the burning barn behind me. It seemed that my senses had conspired to give me a wondrous send-off—all gold and rushing wind. The pain from my shoulder made the scene more real, as if my escape, the idea of it, had been made manifest en mi cuerpo.

"I heard Julio shoot twice more before I was out of range and my cousin's voice had faded into the dull roar of the wind.

"I didn't know where I was going. I knew only that I was free from Julio and that I had a horse and saddle. I felt as if I had earned them. I thought I had punished an evil man, and therefore God had rewarded me with a horse. I didn't realize that Julio had succeeded. His promise to make me hard, to steer me toward a painful journey, had been kept. In time I'm sure he had a bitter laugh at that, that is, if it ever occurred to that mule. He had no sense of irony, you know.

"I rode through the night, fearing that he was following me. I knew he would kill me. It was morning before I stopped. I was in the mountains, and it was cool, not like the heat of Veracruz. I didn't want to climb very high, so I found a comfortable place near the base. In the moonlight I saw that I was at the bottom of Monte Albán. Do you know what that is, boy?" he asked me. I shook my head.

"It is there the Zapotecs built their temples. Great stone temples, standing mute in the dark. I wondered what gods they had entreated there on cool, misty nights long ago. There among the ruins I sat to plan what I would do.

"But what did I know? I was a seventeen-year-old bastard. A true bastard now, having almost killed my "father." I was a bit like you are now, alone, on the move. Silly notions run through your head when you're alone and in pain and darkness engulfs you. That sort of shroud doesn't let in the light of reason. When you're a young man, running seems an end in itself. It doesn't have a destination, that is, a destination that is real or understood. It is very romantic.

"I lay next to my horse and thought foolish thoughts. I would become a bandido, robbing in the city, living in the mountains. But this mountain did not look like a place where I wanted to live. I did not want to live a sacred life. I wanted to live an exciting life. Soon, as eventually happens to all romantics, my fantasy gave way to hunger. My shoulder had turned black and the slightest touch sent agony down my arm. I decided to go on, not to stay at the mountain. I decided to go to Chihuahua and become a caballero.

"I started off late that morning. By the end of the afternoon I had gone through several of the villages that dotted the mountains. Some people were helpful, allowing me to water my horse. But others, human nature being suspicious and unwilling to put itself at risk, turned away when they saw me. I imagined I looked like some demon escaped from hell, all fury and desperation. I probably looked like an orphan who'd stolen a horse from some unfortunate farmer, but couldn't ride and had taken a nasty fall.

"On the second night I got scared. I was no longer driven by the need to escape Julio; I knew he would never find me. The excitement of being free began to wear off as the cold night air of the mountains blew through my coatless body. The paths through the Sierras were dangerous, winding higher and higher, twisting unexpectedly, at some spots only inches from thousand-foot ravines. I was falling asleep on top of the horse. I would awaken, the horse no longer walking, in the middle of a path, only a few feet from death. I finally dismounted and found an alcove in which to spend the night. I tied the horse to a mesquite and fell asleep. But it was difficult to sleep frightened.

"I rode on this way for the next several days. The horse drank water in the villages and ate shrubbery. I was not so fortunate. I drank in the villages, but there were some days I did not eat. I was getting weary. My shoulder was causing me great pain. When I asked for directions to Chihuahua, I got no answer or I was told it was many days away.

"Somehow I arrived in Oaxaca. I think I was dying. I had a fever, and I could no longer move my arm. I was imagining things. The road swerved in front of me even though I knew it was straight. That's when I came to the old man's farm.

"He fed me and nursed my shoulder. But he did something more important than that. He told me the truth, Luis. He told me I would never make it to Chihuahua. He liked me. He told me of his son who had left many years before, left him to die a blind old man. I didn't ask him why his son left and he didn't tell me. At first all he would volunteer was that he had been "adventurous."

"In the next weeks, I rested. The old man was patient and didn't ask me many questions about how I'd managed to dislocate my shoulder. He walked about sightlessly, but he didn't use a stick. He knew his place perfectly. From room to room, he'd pass with ease. One might not have guessed his affliction had they witnessed him only in his own house. I'd watch him walk to the well with a bucket and fill it with water, spilling nothing as he walked back. He had a few chickens and an old plowhorse that no longer plowed, or did much of anything for that matter. The old man would feed them and then himself. For the rest of the day he'd sit in front of the house, getting up now and then to walk about and stretch. He seemed to me very lonely. It's awful to lose one's sight. I'd lose any other sense rather than that one.

"When I was well enough to get around without too much trouble, I offered to help him as payment for his hospitality. 'You can't see, but you need repairs on your fence and your chicken coop is falling apart. The chickens don't want to live in it,' I told him.

" 'What do I care what the chickens want? I'll eat them soon enough if they think their troubles have become too much to bear. As for my fence, my neighbor is dead and my horse Moctezuma, he's too old to wander anywhere. I think he celebrated when I went blind. He knew he would be able to retire. You go fixing the fence and you might scare him to death.'

"But I went to work on the old man's farm. He said nothing more about my work, but he took to cooking my meals and providing me with good company. After a few months had passed, the place resembled a decent farm. I still planned to leave as soon as I could, but it was comfortable there. I got to like the old man considerably. He didn't say much, but he listened to my ideas and my dreams. One day he asked me flat out, 'Where are your people? Why don't you go back to them?'

"I told him how I had been sold by my father. 'That is a difficult thing to learn so young,' he said. 'But I suppose you were bound to learn it sooner or later. Most of us are peones, working off our debts in one way or another. The fucking thing is, we often have to work others' debts off as well. You're damned lucky if you work only toward your own freedom. Of course, that's illusion as well. In this life someone is bound to own you, and more than likely you won't be treated fairly. Like most, you won't even be aware of when you've paid your debt. You just go on paying. It's a good thing you finally realized. But this wandering around, it won't do you any good. You'll slow down, maybe go blind like me, or worse, lose the use of your legs or arms. What then? What good would your trips and adventures do you? Look at me. I'm blind and useless to anyone but myself. But I have my place, old and run-down as it is. All this adventuring, it's brought nothing but death, disease, and pain since the beginning of history.

" 'My son Juan, he left years ago. He's probably dead by now. He left in search of some mischief. No doubt he found it. He thought himself Hernán Cortés, longing for his own personal Mexico, as many brash young men do. Pendejo. Now, I don't accuse you of this. You had to leave. But when you find a place that offers you a home, a haven, don't be so foolish as to turn your horse and run.'

"He seemed to me a wise old prophet. I took to calling myself his son, and people in the village believed me. I was content there. He was right. But then the old man got sick. He took leave of his senses at times. On the night of his death, he began calling for his son. I thought he meant me, so I went to him. But he didn't recognize me. He thought I was Juan, his flesh and blood son. I told him who I was, but he couldn't understand. He took my hand.

" 'Juan,' he began, 'I forgive you. It's your birthright. It's your birthright.' He repeated this until the fever made him sleep.

"He didn't wake up. I buried him the next morning. I knew no one in the town cared much whether he lived or died. I prayed for his soul. That's all I could do. You must understand that all I had was that farm. It was mine. I had worked hard for it, taking care of the old man and the farm, planting and selling the produce for two years.

"Then there was Elisa. I met her in the mercado in El Tlacolula. I had heard that on Sundays it was the best place to sell corn. There they still speak Zapotec, which I did not know. Elisa helped me to bargain when she saw how helpless I was. Her father owned a large section in the mercado. He didn't like me, and it's certain he only allowed me to see her because of my farm. She was afraid of her father. She respected the stupid goat, as our women are taught to do. I went and spoke with him. I asked for her hand and he agreed, but without that farm he would not have allowed the marriage. It was all I could offer. That's why I had to kill the old man's son."

"He came back?"

"Yes, that cabrón. He came back a few days before my wedding. He came to see his father, to claim the farm. And I only days from marrying my Elisa."

Berto stopped. "I will finish later. I'm exhausted." His head dropped as he found sleep. I listened to him muttering the name of his wife, lifting his head, realizing she was not there, his eyes wide open, staring into the darkness, focusing on something seen only by him.

*   *   *

Two men died during the third day. I didn't know them. I had only heard their voices. The other men had stopped moving and talking. Everyone sat or lay against the walls, breathing shallowly. A few of the men were now drinking their own urine.

I dreamt that a voice begged Pablo to cut the dead men's hands and feet off so the living could drink their blood. Pablo stood drunkenly and, staggering to the fresh corpses, he struck the hands and feet from the first one and the head from the other. Five or six of the men drank.

"Will you drink?" a voice demanded.

"Who?"

"Drink if you love your life."

"I won't do that."

"Then you'll die."

"What's happening in here?" I asked. "When the hell will we arrive?"

"The coyote has gone insane."

"What are you talking about? There is no coyote in here," I said.

"Pablo. He is the coyote. He has been put on this boxcar to watch us. Why do you think we have an axe in here? He is the killer on this trip. By now he is possessed by the devil.

Soon he will start killing live ones for their blood. He is your judgment. See him, el diablo, el coyote. See his fierce eyes? It isn't madness. It's all the hatred, all the pain of these men, right there, focused. Your creation. Don't get too close to him. He'll bite you, infect you too."

"Who are you?" I asked.

"I am the part of you that never sleeps."

I saw Pablo. He was drunk with blood, his face smeared red, his mouth slightly open. I saw him as a Spaniard, a conquistador. Hernán Cortés willing to burn his ships, to sacrifice all. Satanic, a living blasphemy believing himself hidden from the sight of God. He slowly began to taste his lips, his tongue obscenely licking the last of the moist blood. A wild man howling without making a sound. His body could not contain the evil spirit that possessed him and drifted thickly, surrounding him, his shape obscured and hazy.

\*　\*　\*

The heat in the car raged. It seemed worse than ever before. I imagined I was in hell, in a dark, death-smelling hell. My tongue was beginning to swell; every swallow I made sent fire down my throat. I couldn't stand it anymore. I stuck my hand into my bedroll and very slowly unscrewed the cap of my canteen. I stuck my index finger down into it. The canteen was almost full. I had only taken one drink. Carefully I lifted the wet finger to my mouth. A single drop rolled down onto the tip of my dry tongue and was instantly absorbed. I rubbed the rest of the moisture on my blistered lips. As I did so, I almost lost control. I pictured myself lifting the canteen to my mouth and pouring a stream of water down my throat, a wave of cool, clear water filling my dusty mouth. I saw the water gushing from the canteen, my mouth overflowing, rivulets running down my chin onto my chest. I was ready to die for it now. I gripped the canteen tightly, and as I began to lift it, my eyes fell upon Pablo. He was looking in my direction. My hand fumbled, and I felt precious water run into my bedroll. Only a mouthful spilled, but I had to stifle a cry.

I waited for him to look away from me, and then I recapped the canteen. I wrung as much water as I could from the cloth, and quickly wiped my hand across my mouth. The water evaporated almost before I could run my tongue across my lips.

"Do you know what I am going to do first when I get out of here?" I whispered to Berto.

He did not respond.

"I'm going to drink so much water that cupfuls will squirt from my nose."

# Chapter Seven

Berto was beginning to die. I knew by listening to him. He no longer spoke in whispers, afraid that others would hear. His chin rested against his chest, so that it appeared as if he were talking to his knees spread open before him.

"A man must always consider everything he does. What does it profit a man to gain the world if he loses his soul? Nothing! That was my sin, gaining the world. A world of cattle and a farm with a world of corn. Now I am in hell. En el infierno con el diablo."

Pablo did not move. He did not even glance in the old man's direction.

"He pretends not to hear me," Berto said. "Do you see?"

"Be still," I said. "If he does hear you there's no telling what he'll do."

"I don't care. I don't care. It'll happen anyway and if it happens now, then that's how it's supposed to be." He lifted his head, turning toward me as if he had just learned something surprising. "You're scared. Yes. You're scared. Do you have something to confess? You do! Everyone in this box is here for judgment. That's the explanation. Nothing happens without some purpose, isn't that right? What is it that you did, then? Out with it, boy."

"You have a fever, old man. I haven't done anything to confess except for being idiot enough to walk into this box."

"Stupidity is the greatest sin of all. Now you see. This is your comeuppance. Stupidity, that is the worst. I know. I myself was stupid enough to be deceived. I murdered my wife and child. Listen," he said, grasping my arm. "It was in the middle of the day. I had finished watering the corn, and I was resting in the chair the old man used to sit in. From where I sat I could see the road. Two men came riding slowly toward the farm. I paid no attention, for it was common for people to travel that road to town for provisions. But these men didn't pass my farm. They stopped in front of my house and dismounted.

" 'Where is Don Vargas?' the tall one asked.

" 'He's dead. I'm his son and this is now my farm. If you have any business with Don Vargas, you may address me.'

"The tall man was surprised. I could tell by the way he looked at the short, silent one, but he did not act surprised. Instead he smiled. He was the old man's son.

" 'I don't remember a brother. It's curious.' He surveyed the grounds slowly. 'What have you done with my father? Did you kill him and then steal his farm? Is his grave somewhere out there in those cornfields? Now you're trying to act like his son, hoping no one will discover. Did my father tell you I was dead or never coming back? Or are you just a squatter?'

" 'No,' " I said, 'you're wrong. I did not kill your father. I too am his son, a bastard. I took care of him. He gave me this farm with his dying breath.'

"He looked at me for a moment, and then he smiled.

" 'Well, bastard son, my father couldn't read or write, and dying breaths are not legal. You must know that I, as legitimate son, am entitled to this farm.'

"I remembered the old man's words giving his son his birthright. But I couldn't leave. I had worked hard. That man had left his father. Didn't the old man call me his son? I was to marry Elisa in a few days. I knew her father wouldn't let us marry if I was chased off my farm like a dog. I decided to kill him. Wouldn't you have done the same? He was going to take my farm! Elisa would not be mine. I had to kill him, no?

I nodded my head slowly. Berto watched me closely, as if he were trying to remember my face. And then he began again. "I pretended to leave. Even knowing what I had in mind, that act was almost unbearable. Juan and the man entered my home holding a vulgar conversation, picking things up, stopping only to comment on the value of objects that caught their eye. 'Ándale, hermanito,' Juan mocked me, 'you better be riding off soon. We don't want an Abel and Cain re-enactment here.' I threw together some things rapidly. They didn't say anything when I left. They stood on the porch and watched. I rode off quickly, fearing they would shoot me in the back. I rode until I was out of sight of the farm. You know, it didn't occur to me to challenge him at all. I left without so much as a complaint.

"I tied my horse to a tree and waited. When it was dark I began to walk back to the farm. It was a long walk, but because I wanted to kill the men in their sleep, it suited my purpose. As I walked, the old man's dying words began to weigh me down. But I didn't listen. I kept walking.

"When I got to the house, it was dark. I checked the barn to see if the men's horses were still there. Juan's was there, but the short man's was gone. The horse neighed quietly as I took a machete from the wall. My hand trembled as I gripped the leather handle. I walked out of the barn and headed for the house. The moon was bright, and the glimmer of the machete's blade flickered in my eyes. I began to get things straight in my head. It takes concentration and clear purpose to kill. I knew it was a serious thing. And I also knew that I was a coward to sneak into his bed and murder him in his sleep.

"I came to the door of the house and opened it slowly, so as not to make any noise. The door gave way silently, and I entered. The house seemed airless, very quiet, so much so that I could hear my own breathing. The only light came from under the shades covering the windows. I walked through the parlor, my feet making the floor creak ever so slightly, every sound making my heart tremble. I was losing my nerve. I think I would have turned around had I not been so far into the house.

"As I moved toward the room in which he slept, my eyes followed a ray of moonlight past the doorway. It fell on the man's face, exposing his mouth. He was not asleep. He was sitting in the old man's wooden chair. 'You've come to kill me, have you?' he said. 'You've come like a thief, a coward, in the middle of the night to kill me while I sleep.'

" 'Yes, I've come to kill you in your bed. I was going to slit your throat and let you drown in your own blood, like a pig. Como un marrano.'

" 'And you, my brother. How would Father feel about you killing me for what is rightfully mine?' he mocked me.

" 'I am more of a son to him than you ever were. I took care of him. He gave me this land as reward for my faithfulness, and now you come like a thief to take it, knowing the law will give it to you because you bear his name. I am making my own law.' I was getting very angry. He seemed, sitting there, more than my enemy. He was a thief, but so was I, and I realized that I was like him, that we might indeed have kindred souls.

" 'You see, I know the old man never fathered another son. He spent his whole miserable life on this farm, drinking himself blind and counting on me staying here and caring for him until he decided to die. I didn't expect him to be dead yet; I thought he would certainly be alive to torment me further, shaming me into begging him for forgiveness. It has turned out very well. You've turned this hovel into a good farm. I'm going to sell it for a good price, and then I'm never coming back to this desert.'

"I stood there, rage building inside me. 'You're going to sell this farm to that man you came with?'

" 'No, that man is my partner. And you, my brother, have become a nuisance. I'm not sure I can let you go now. I don't think you'll leave things as they should be.'

"I heard him pull back the hammer of a pistol. 'If you leave now, I won't kill you. You must understand, my brother, that I have a family, a wife and children, many responsibilities. I would rather kill you, a usurper in the house of my father, than cause my family any discomfort or harm. I don't know how you came here. I'm sure he welcomed you with open arms, but now he's dead. Now I'm here. This is mine and I'm taking it.'

"He was no longer taunting me. I could hear the sincerity in his voice. I could have left, Luis, but instead I stood there paralyzed like a fool. I can lie to you and say that it was a matter of pride, that I had been pushed as far as a man can be pushed, but it was not so. I was scared. I was sure that when I turned to leave, he would shoot me in the back. I heard it in his voice. He, too, was a coward. He couldn't shoot me face to face. He wanted me to turn so he wouldn't have to look at me.

" 'I've warned you, Brother. I've given you a choice. Surely you're not such a fool as to want to die for this miserable piece of dirt. You're young, you have no family. You can build yourself another farm, another life. Turn around and I'll give you that chance.'

"I didn't move. I stood there watching him. He slowly brought the gun up into the light so that I could see it aimed at me. His finger was on the trigger, his mouth was slightly open, and he was running his tongue over his lips nervously.

" 'You knew I was coming back tonight. Your friend didn't believe you and went to get drunk in town, and so you sat here waiting for me in the dark, planning to kill me when I walked in. But you're as much a coward as I am. You can't shoot me in the face. You want me to turn around so you can shoot me in the back. You want the easy way out once again, Juan. You couldn't stay here with your father. You left, hoping you could make a life for yourself elsewhere, and you have failed. Why did you come back? To beg your father's forgiveness?' Then I understood. 'No. You came back to kill him and take the farm, didn't you? That's why you brought that man. You couldn't bear to kill your father with your own hands. You had to bring someone else to carry out your plan.'

"That's when he shot me. I felt fire run through my hand. I jumped across the room and into the hall. I put my hand between my legs. I could feel my pants getting soaked with my blood. I lifted my hand to my face. In the dim light I could see that half of it had been blown off. Through the torn skin and all the blood I could see a white bone sticking out crookedly. It had been my finger. Nausea overcame me, and I began to wretch. The bleeding wouldn't stop.

" 'I'm just going to wait here with my gun. You'll be dead in a few minutes. And then you'll be no more trouble. Accusing me of killing my own father for this dirt,' he yelled.

"I could hear him coming. He wasn't sure he had shot me, and he wanted to make sure. I waited there in the darkness, listening to his slow, cautious footsteps. I still held the machete in my good hand. Standing slowly, I raised the blade, waiting for him to round the corner and come past the doorway where I stood ready. He heard me and fired at the doorway. I didn't move again because I thought I would faint. I stood there, trying not to breathe, ignoring the blood that was puddling at my feet. He walked toward the doorway. He was now so close that I could hear his rapid, shallow breathing. He stopped a foot from the door, too petrified to move.

" 'Maldito,' I heard him say.

"He started to walk forward again, and as he did I sprang, forcing the machete into his throat. He was so surprised that he brought both hands to his neck, dropping the gun without firing it. I pulled the blade from his neck as I fell back against the wall, sliding down onto the floor. Juan kept his hands at his throat, tightening his grip, trying to slow the bleeding. In the moonlight, I could see the blood streaming down his neck, little bubbles surfacing in the flow from the gash that went through his windpipe. Slowly, his knees began to buckle, and he fell to the floor. He gasped for air as he choked on his own blood.

"I took off my belt, tying it tightly around my wrist. The bleeding slowed, some of it already beginning to crust. I sat there waiting in the dark, not having the strength to get up. With my foot, I dragged the gun to my hand. I picked it up, holding it in readiness. But nothing happened, and I eventually fell asleep.

"The pain woke me up. It was still dark in the house. The pain scourged my arm from my hand to my neck. I tried to lift it, but it brought tears to my eyes. The pain was so intense I couldn't stop myself from moaning. And then I heard a horse riding up to the barn. It was the other man. He was angry, cursing at the horse, thrusting open the barn door. I heard him come through the front door.

" 'Juan, did he come back?' he yelled.

"He didn't say anything else. I think he smelled the blood. I couldn't see very well, but I squinted my eyes, readying the gun. He came into the hallway cautiously. He saw the body and began walking toward it slowly. I cocked the trigger, pulling the gun up so that I could shoot him as he stepped through the doorway. He stopped in front of Juan's body, looking directly into the barrel of the gun.

" 'You're going to kill me? I don't even have a gun.' He didn't say it pleadingly; he sounded as if he were just stating a common fact.

" 'You came to kill the old man,' I said.

" 'No. He came to kill the old man.'

" 'Now you thought you would find that Juan had killed me and both of you could bury me. Was that your plan?'

"The man's face changed. His gaze dropped. He did not want me to see his fear.

" 'You're scared because you know that I can kill you, that I should kill you,' I said.

" 'Don't kill me,' he said softly.

" 'What did you say?' I asked.

" 'Don't kill me.' This time he said it louder.

"I don't know what took hold of me, God help me. I can say that it was the pain or the fever but, no, it was the devil.

" 'You don't want to die, is that it?' I said.

" 'No.' He looked toward the window.

"The sun was beginning to rise, turning the room pale gray.

" 'You think I should spare you because you didn't try to kill me. You think I should let you go, ride off, back to your home as if you didn't come here looking to rob me of everything?'

" 'If you're going to kill me, then shoot me,' he said.

"I shot into the roof. The man covered his head and began to tremble.

" 'Oh, you're scared now? Look at me,' I said, holding out my ruined hand, the roar of pain enraging me more.

" 'I'll leave. I won't come back. He didn't tell me he was coming to kill the old man. He told me he had some land he would sell to me for a good price. My family . . .' He stopped.

" 'Does your family know you were going to kill an old man to buy his home for a good price?'

" 'I tell you, they didn't know. I didn't know.' His voice was beginning to crack. 'Please,' he said softly. He wouldn't look into my face. He dropped to his knees and began to cry.

" 'You're a coward,' I said. 'That's why you left when that cabrón told you I would be back. You wanted him to kill me while you were away so you wouldn't have to share in his guilt, just as you would have done had the old man been here.'

" 'No, no. You don't . . . no, I was going to . . . I have a family, and they . . . don't . . . ,' he said brokenly.

"I stared at him crying, both of his hands resting on his knees. I felt no remorse, none. I saw only Julio, and I saw him telling me that men must fear you, and then I knew.

" 'Do you fear me?' I asked him. For the first time he looked into my eyes. He said nothing, but I saw that he did not truly fear me.

" 'Do you fear me? Answer me,' I demanded.

"He looked thoughtful, and then it seemed as if relief shone from his eyes. He began to nod slowly. 'Yes,' he said loudly, 'yes!'

"And then I shot him in the head. He fell backwards onto the floor, dead by the time his head struck the wood planks. I sat there looking at the two men I had killed, feeling tired and yet powerful . . . proud that I had taken their lives as they'd wanted to take my life and my land. I felt as if I'd won something. Yes, as if I'd won my freedom again. It was the same feeling I'd had as I rode away from Julio, leaving his barn and his profits in flames. I was proud! Proud that I had just damned myself, selling my soul for power. I didn't care then.

"As I recovered at my Elisa's home, her father came to see me. 'Do you know what you've done?' he asked me.

" 'Yes, I defended my land from two thieves—'

" 'Yes, I know very well. Two thieves. Two thieves who fought for Madero in the revolution. Two thieves the people would look on as heroes and who are bound to have told the gang they led where they were going. That was the old man's son. He returned to take the farm back, didn't he?'

" 'Yes, he was his son, but he was not here to raise money for the revolution. He was here to take the land away from me after I took care of the old man and worked on—'

" 'Don't you see that it doesn't matter?' he yelled. 'The people of this town won't care about the old man. They only know that the two dead men fought on behalf of the campesinos, the agrarians, the peasants, in order to help Madero defeat Díaz. Now that Huerta has assassinated Madero, the people are angry. They are beginning to rise again in the north under Villa and in the South under Zapata. The revolution will soon start again, and what have you done? You've killed two revolutionaries, two heroes.'

" 'Who knows?' I asked.

" 'Everyone will know soon enough. The malcriados who buried them have probably been in the cantina spreading the word every night since they found out.'

" 'But what will the people of this town do? They know me. They know I'm no político. They won't kill me,' I said.

"Had I known that it would be my wife and daughter who would suffer, I never would have married Elisa. I would have run instead. I would have gone to the mountains and hid. No, better, I would have hidden in a black box like this where the devil could punish me without touching those I loved."

Berto stopped talking. His chin dropped against his chest once again and he slept. I tried to occupy my mind by calculating the time that had passed since I had first stepped onto the train. I no longer remembered. It seemed like months, my old life just a dark memory.

"A dark hole, a grave, Elisa, a grave," Berto mumbled.

# Chapter Eight

I am in a tunnel long enough that I cannot see its end, and yet I have traveled so far inside that I can no longer see its beginning.

"I am hallucinating," I hear a voice from the tunnel say. This voice is faint. Someone has spoken from far beyond where I now lie. I don't listen. Instead I stand up and begin to walk.

"What are you trying to find?" the same voice asks.

"My father," I say.

"Liar!"

"No. It's the truth."

"You hated him. That's why you ran," the voice says. The voice is joined by others: "Yes, that's true. You sang praises at his death. Inside yourself you rejoiced at his dying. He would never lock you in the dark again, and you were glad."

"No. It was the dark I hated, not him. He taught me to—"

"To cringe in the darkness like a coward!"

"No. Where am I?"

"You are here in the darkness to face your devil. Your father. He's here. He's waiting somewhere in the darkness for you, to lock you up."

I walk around in circles. Scurrying sounds, like rats, surround me. I want to run, but I'm afraid of running into him. I hear an axe chopping into the trunk of a tree, then the screams of a man dying in the darkness, crying for María. Moans come from all sides. I fear that if I step behind me, I'll step on a man or, before me, on a squealing rat.

"If he gets any closer, he'll know you're afraid of the dark" the voice says.

"Who?" I ask.

"The one who put you here."

"Who? Why?"

"Your father," the voice continues. "He wants to see if his son is scared of the dark . . . of the devil. Can you cut down the tree?"

"I'm not afraid," I say softly.

I hear nothing.

"I'm not afraid," I say, louder.

I hear nothing.

"He did lock me up!"

I see pale light drifting from above. Heat is beginning to consume me. The moans are louder now.

*   *   *

I awoke, my tongue so swollen that it was now too large for my mouth and stuck out past my lips. I imagined it made me look like a dog holding a piece of rotting meat in its snout. I could no longer avoid the stench by breathing through my mouth. Painfully, the heat scorched my nostrils. The air seemed to have tiny bristles that scraped my dry throat.

"The itch," a man groaned. "Oh, oh, oh. The itch. My whole body. It itches."

It was thirst. He was dying. The dehydration scourged his flesh with its gnawing teeth. He began to scratch himself violently, his fingernails digging into his skin, which came away in strips. Blood seeped across his face, then across his chest and arms. He tore at himself for another hour, at times bringing his own blood to his bloated tongue, thinking it was water. Then he died.

I could no longer tell how many of the men were dead. Berto was still breathing, and I could see Pablo still holding the axe. There were a few groans, and I could hear someone weeping on the other side of the box. I could think of only one thing—the man's tears. His moist tears rolling down into his mouth.

I looked over at Pablo. He had not moved since I had awakened. I reached into my bedroll, taking the canteen in my hand. Opening it slowly, I lifted it to my lips, pressing its open mouth to my swollen tongue. I kept my knees up, and tilted the bottle slightly, not wanting to make a sound. A tiny stream of water ran into my mouth as I lifted the rim of the canteen. I almost choked as the fluid ran down my throat. I lifted the rim again, this time longer. Water filled my mouth, and I fought the urge to gulp it down. Instead, I kept the water in my mouth, letting it quench the dryness of my tongue, allowing only a rivulet at a time to run down my throat. I took one more drink and put the canteen away again.

I began to feel nauseated as soon as the water reached my stomach. My abdomen and legs cramped, wanting more. I was afraid I would vomit. The smell of the rotting bodies was overwhelming, but until now the thirst had kept me from noticing. Those two drinks of water seemed to rouse my sense of smell.

I tore a long section of my undershirt away, wrapping it across my face. The poisoned air still seeped through the cloth, but not as strongly, and I was able to keep from vomiting. I could hear a man heaving somewhere to my left. He was not throwing up. He had nothing to vomit. He just heaved, sounding like someone was punching him in the stomach. After more retching, a liquid poured from his mouth. The bitter smell of bile cut through the sweet stench of decay. After a few minutes he stopped. He turned on his back and lay panting.

"When will this damned train start moving again!" yelled Alejandro. "We're all dying of thirst, and my eye . . . it's all infected . . . it's rotting in my face. Where in hell are we?"

He was talking to Pablo, but Pablo did not even turn toward him.

"Rosales, that bastard. Fuck his children. He told us we'd be in Texas soon. Now here we are . . . where? Pablo? Where in hell are we?"

Alejandro stood shakily. "Where, cabrón! Answer me. You think you don't have to answer me, Pablo," he said, stumbling as he walked. "You think you don't have to talk to me because you're the fucking 'coyote'? Well, I'm a goddamn wolf. So what the fuck? Remember Rosales put both of us here. Answer me, goddamn you!"

Pablo did not look up. He stared ahead as if in a trance, as if he were dreaming, pictures floating in front of his face.

"The stench," Alejandro said. "It's driven you crazy. It's making me crazy. We'll all be dead if we don't get out of here."

At last Pablo spoke. "You silly pendejo. You think you know anything about what's happening in here? Take care you don't disturb me enough to make me have to expend any energy. You should sit down and save the little strength you seem to possess. You'll need it so they won't have to pull your carcass out with the rest of them when this train stops."

Alejandro did not sit. "How in the hell am I supposed to do that? My goddamned eye is dripping puss. It's running down my face like fucking tears. My eye is rotting! I need water and someone to take a look at me. I didn't join this god-forsaken trip to die. This fucking stench, this fucking blood. You've got to let us out now."

Pablo seemed undisturbed by Alejandro's pleas. "When I was a boy, my father took me to see a dog fight. They were big, and the men who held them had ropes tied around the dogs' throats. They had to keep a tight grip on the ropes, almost choking the dogs. The dogs would lunge at each other, trying to get free so they could rip each others' throats out. One of the men had thrown a hen into his dog's cage. The dog had gone mad, it seemed to me. He ripped the chicken into bloody pieces, chewing its body to pulp. He was vicious, that dog. He was foaming by the time his master had him in the pit. Ready to fight. This dog was covered in blood, howling, ready to tear into his master's leg. He was frenzied. The other dog pulled at his rope, but he didn't bark or bare his teeth. He kept quiet, keeping the rope taut, staring at the mad dog.

" 'You see the quiet one?' my father asked me. 'You see how earnestly he stares at the other dog? Tell me, who do you think will win?'

" 'The bloody dog,' I said.

" 'No, no. Look at the quiet dog's eyes. He's not mad, he's not frothing at the mouth for blood. He doesn't like to kill, but he's not afraid. Look at him.'

"The men let the dogs loose. The bloody one sprang at the quiet dog, pumping his legs, his lips pulled back, his teeth snapping. The other dog seemed to wait, motionless. The son of a bitch was planning. When the bloody dog lunged at him, he backed away quickly, leaving the bloody dog off balance, and before the bloody dog could regain his position, the quiet dog had pounced on him. He sank his teeth into the throat of the bloody dog, locking his jaws, not chewing. He bore down on the other dog and waited for him to stop struggling.

"It was over very quickly. Many men lost money. My father won almost a thousand pesos. As we were leaving I heard the owner of the dead dog talking to his friend. 'I don't understand. My dog, he was purebred, powerful. His jaws, you've seen them . . . I don't see how he could have lost to that mongrel.' His friend shook his head.

"I asked my father how he knew, and do you know what he said, Alejandro? He said, 'You can't let the blood make you crazy.' When there's vicious work to be done, to survive you must keep your head." Pablo motioned toward the floor with his chin. "Now, sit down, fool."

"We're all going to die," Alejandro whispered.

"No, not all of us will. I won't. Every bastard in this box may rot, but I'll walk away when those cabrones open the door in Texas. When they open the doors. Do you hear, Alejandro? They. This axe is for one thing only. It won't open any door."

Alejandro sat back down.

# Chapter Nine

It had been quiet since Alejandro's argument with Pablo. I didn't know how many men were still alive, but no one was making a sound. The heat was still oppressive, the night being at least an hour away. Then someone began to moan. At first it was soft, almost soothing to me, but then he began to get louder, sometimes shrieking. I couldn't understand what he said. He would stop suddenly, but only for a few moments, and then he would begin again. The shrieks grew more piercing and horrible. It seemed as if the man were being burned alive.

"Shut him up," someone said.

But no one did anything. I didn't know if anyone knew the man. Finally, Chico stood up and walked over to him. "Shut up!" he yelled. "Shut your filthy mouth!"

The man didn't seem to hear him. He kept screaming. Chico wrapped his hands around the man's throat and began to strangle him. The man kept trying to scream but only made little gasps until he died.

\*   \*   \*

"Tell me something happy," Berto said.

His words surprised me. He had not spoken to me in several hours. I had even begun to fear that the old man was dead.

"What do you want me to tell you?" I asked.

"Something funny . . . happy," he said.

"About when we get to Texas?"

"No. You don't know anything about Texas. Tell me something happy about Bustamante . . . about your father . . . or your grandmother . . . anything. But it must be real."

I tried to think. All good memories seemed so far away and inaccessible to me in that dark box. I closed my eyes and I saw something I had not thought about in years. "My grandmother made my first piñata. It was in the shape of a donkey. It wasn't very big, but it was very colorful. It was orange and red, its tail purple, its eyes green, the ears different colors. I didn't know I was going to get one. I was only four. It was so beautiful. My father hung it on a tree and handed me a stick. 'You break it,' he said.

"But I didn't want to break it. It had so many colors. It was swinging back and forth from the rope. I thought it was dancing. I didn't want to hit the donkey. It was too happy, dancing up in the tree. 'No,' I said.

" 'You have to if you want the candy and presents inside the donkey. Hit it.'

"I started to cry. I threw the stick to the ground and ran to my grandmother, who was sitting watching me. 'You don't have to hit it. You don't want to hurt your donkey?'

" 'No,' I said.

"She told my father to lower the piñata. She took the candy and toys from inside without breaking him."

"What happened to the donkey?" asked Berto.

"I kept it for years in my room. I finally lost it."

"But you didn't break it. That's nice. That's happy. Tell me something else happy. It can be anything."

"I can't think of anything else right now," I said.

"It doesn't have to be true then," Berto said. "Tell me about Texas."

I closed my eyes and imagined Texas. "It won't be so hot. When they open the door to this boxcar, the air will hit us and the stench in here will fly away. We'll climb out and forget the smell of blood and death, and the air will feel cool. We'll feel a breeze and it will invigorate us. We'll know we're there and we're still alive. And water . . . ahhh . . . water everywhere. Rivers and rivers of water. Imagine it. Here we are crossing to Texas on a railroad when we could have gone by river! But when we get there, we'll find one. Maybe when we pick we can make our camp on the banks of one. When we come home hot and tired, we can take off our dirty rags and jump in for a swim. You know, that would be much better than the ocean even, because you can drink and swim at the same time. At night, we'll be so close to the bank that the water's murmur will sing us to sleep. Very poetic, no?"

"Yes, very poetic," Berto said, sounding unconvinced. "I can assure you of one thing, I'll never get on a goddamned train again."

"We won't have to. We'll go in trucks or even by foot. The work will be hard, but the boss'll be fair. Unless that bastard Rosales is around. If he is, we'll leave. What can he do anyway? I hear there are lots of crops to choose from. I prefer apples or oranges. That way you're in the shade and above the ground. When you get hungry I don't think anyone will mind if you eat an apple. Of course, apples and oranges are a heavy crop. Maybe tomatoes. Anything except cotton or corn. With cotton, you cut up your fingers, and with corn, you itch. But I guess we can start with whatever work we can get. The important thing is to work for a good person. At the end of the week we'll get American money and go eat at a restaurant, but not Mexican food, American food . . . only maybe once in a while Mexican food. Maybe when I'm homesick, but I'm curious about the food there. I've heard you can buy food whenever you're hungry. You can get any kind of food there, too. There's even more choices there than in Mexico City. You can get food from China, France, Russia, anywhere, but I think I'll try the American food first.

"You know, if we stick together and pool our money we can save and find a house. When we get there you'll feel better. It's this trip that's taken your energy. All you need is a place to rest up, some water, some food, then you'll be fine. Maybe we'll meet up with other Mexicanos and we can share the costs and still afford to help our families back home. Texas is like heaven. You'll start all over. Once we're over there, it'll all be new."

Berto didn't say anything.

"You need a drink," I said, nudging him. "I have water in my canteen," I whispered. "Look, it's almost night. Soon there won't be any light in here. When it's pitch black, I'll hand you the water."

\*   \*   \*

It was dark. I waited until I thought Pablo was asleep. I was very anxious. It occurred to me that the old man might die before I could get to him. When I couldn't wait any longer, I took the canteen from the bedroll and unscrewed the cap. Berto took it from my hands gently. He only took one drink and then handed it back.

"Don't waste it on a dead man," he said.

"Don't be stupid," I whispered, "We'll be there soon. Be smart. Drink enough to keep you alive until we get there."

"Do you want to hear my happiest day?"

"Yes," I said.

"I was a boy. I was watching my father repair a barrel for a neighbor. My father was complaining that the staves of the barrel were almost all rotten and the barrel would be better used as firewood. I didn't say anything; I just watched. It was hot that day and my father was tired and grouchy. He had already told me to stay out of his way and keep quiet. Finally, as he seemed ready to give up on the barrel, he stood back and looked at me. 'Go get me a blanket, a heavy one,' he said. I got the heaviest one in the house and ran with it dragging behind me. When I gave it to him, he padded the barrel with it. Then he picked up the barrel and we walked to a hill. We had many hills where I lived. 'Get in,' he said. Then he rolled me down the hill. I spun around and around all the way down. It was something for me to have the world spinning just above my head. My father, he wasn't much for playing games or giving me rides on his back. I was very sorry when the barrel came to a stop. I thought it was over. But to my surprise my father came down the hill and carried the barrel up again. He rolled me down the hill again and again, taking pleasure in my silly laughter. I remember him laughing, too. My dizziness made it seem like a dream. In this boxcar, it certainly seems like a dream. Anyway, my mother ran out of the house when she heard my delighted screams. She thought I was in trouble. She stood there and stared at us both as if we were crazy. My father even asked her if she wanted a ride. She didn't, but she let us play that afternoon. That's one of the last good things I can remember about them."

"That's sad," I couldn't help saying.

"Sad? Well, yes. But it's better than anything else I can remember, and those are the moments you hold onto."

I took a drink of water and put the canteen away. After a while, I don't know how long, I fell asleep. I dreamt I was in a barrel, rolling and rolling, never coming to a stop. When I woke up, the train was moving again and Berto was shaking me.

# Chapter Ten

"Luis," Berto said, "I must finish now."

"Finish your story?" I asked.

"My confession," he said. "It pains me. I can't help but see it all again in this darkness. It runs before my eyes like an old tragic movie. I see her face and then . . . Look . . ." He pointed at Pablo. "He's listening. That devil's taking pleasure in all this. He's enjoying my tale."

I looked at Pablo, who didn't seem to be awake. He sat on the bale of hay, his eyes closed.

"If I could kill him," Berto said.

"Tell me, Berto.

He began again, but this time he spoke softly, every few moments turning to see if Pablo was listening. "There was grumbling in the town after I got well. The people didn't like having the killer of two 'revolutionaries' living in their midst, but no one ever told me this to my face. They were scared of a man who had killed two men single-handedly. So I was left alone. Elisa loved me, and we were married despite her father's protests. No one came to our wedding. Elisa pretended not to care, but it was painful for her to start her life with me in that way. When I went into town, the men avoided me. Elisa quit coming with me because of the ugly looks.

" 'It doesn't matter, Berto,' she would say. 'Why should I care what those ignorant old women think? It's you I care about. You're all the company I need or want.' I wanted to believe her. What man wouldn't? Maybe I deluded myself into thinking we could go on like this. If I had been more concerned for her welfare, maybe I would have sold the farm and moved away where no one knew us."

"What happened then?"

"We were very content for the next few months. Elisa got pregnant. The farm was coming along well. But the revolution was starting again. There were fierce skirmishes in the mountains around Mexico City and in Baja. Reports of fighting came more frequently. Thousands of Mexicans were killing each other. But our town was lucky; we weren't near any of the revolutionary centers and kept on with our normal lives. Elisa gave birth that summer. I've told you about my Celia.

"But although we didn't pay attention to the revolution, it raged on. People were displaced. I heard from a relative that my father and mother, old as they were, had fled their home for the U.S. I don't know where they settled or if they even got there. We ignored it all. At night I would come to bed tired, sometimes worried that all was not going well with the farm. Elisa became pregnant again. She would sit calmly and listen to my complaints. Soon she would begin to smile. 'What are you smiling about?' I'd ask.

" 'Oh, nothing, nothing at all,' she would say, still smiling.

"Then I would continue my complaints about the boys stealing from me or goofing off, and her grin would grow broader until, no longer able to control herself, she would begin to giggle.

" 'I don't think it's so funny,' I would say.

"Still smiling, she would take my hand. 'Feel,' she would say, putting my hand on her stomach. 'I think it's a boy this time.'

" 'A boy? A boy who will grow up like me.'

" 'Yes, like you, handsome and strong. He'll run fast, but he'll be short.'

" 'Short like my father?' I'd say.

" 'Yes, but strong. Remember, he'll be strong. What will you give him?' she'd ask.

" 'I will give him a horse. And I will give him this farm, but first the horse.'

" 'Is that all?' she'd whisper.

" 'No, I'll let him make his own choices.'

" 'That's a wonderful thing.'

"It was always warm there with her. I would forget about the workers and the farm. Everything I cared about I found in her arms. I would rest my head upon her breasts and she would stroke my hair until I fell asleep. Sometimes, if I asked, she would sing. She would sing so quietly, as if only I was meant to hear the sweet sounds. I would close my eyes, imagining the song was love, love that could be realized with the senses. I still long for her warmth and softness.

"Then one day in late March, the cold weather behind us, I planned a trip to buy some cattle from a rancher who lived near El Yagal. I was to be gone for only a week. Elisa did not want me to go.

"The day I left I felt uneasy. I considered riding back but decided I would not shame myself by acting like a scared woman. I had business to do." Berto stopped speaking.

"Did you go back home?" I asked.

"No, I went and purchased the cattle for a good price," Berto said.

"When did you leave?"

"Luis," Berto said, "enough now. Perhaps later, when I feel better."

"No. You must finish. They were dead when you returned," I said.

"Yes."

"Your father-in-law too?"

"Yes. Him too. He was the first one I found when I returned to the farm."

"Maybe it wasn't revenge. Perhaps it was only thieves. Did they steal anything?"

"It doesn't matter. I brought it into my home. It was for me."

"What did you do?"

"I . . . buried her, them, my daughter and Elisa, next to Elisa's father. And then I left, but I was afraid."

"Of what?"

"That my family had not been killed by men. I knew that I had willed their deaths, doomed them with my . . . crime."

"But you decided to look for the murderers?"

"Yes, feeling that I would find them and exact a terrible punishment. I couldn't sleep in the house. At night I imagined screams, her screams. I remembered everything about the two men I killed. My sin and my punishment were in that house. The darkness in the house. . . . My bed cold, and outside my family buried in the ground."

"How long did you stay?"

"Only days. I took my gun, a bedroll, and some money and left for Chihuahua. I thought if I could keep moving I might be able to keep ahead of those screams, but I had to sleep and they always caught up with me in the night. Her face, her eyes opened in terror, just as I had found her. I thought, I'll keep ahead of the rage and pain until I catch those bastards and then I'll welcome it. I'll rain it down on their heads, on their souls.

"As I searched I moved north, riding from Oaxaca all the way to Cuidad Juárez. All around me I saw miserable, frightened men and women, entire families, sometimes just women and children alone, all heading north, all of them trying to escape the destruction of the war. No one understands why death has come for them. Everyone was trying to outrun it by going to the U.S. I felt superior to them. I wasn't running from it, I was running toward it.

"I met up with groups of desperate men who stole in order to survive, to feed families displaced by the war. I met with others who welcomed the violence, men like those who killed my family, men who rode the current of death and destruction. I did nothing to stop them. I only wanted to know if they'd been near my farm that terrible day. I was no protector of innocents; I only wanted to avenge my family.

"I never found those responsible, and near the end of the tumult, sometime in 1919 or 1920, I realized I never would find them. I exiled myself, a Moses bound to the desert and wilderness of Sonora, thinking that perhaps the sun might blind my mind's eye to their faces. I wanted my surroundings to mirror my soul. I was drawn to the white missions that sat unconcernedly in the desert, not because I sought God, but because they seemed serene in their sober intensity. Blank, reflecting nothing, aware of nothing. But memory does not evaporate. It remains protected from the heat and fury of life. One's lifeblood nourishes it. Only death brings an end . . . only death."

"Did you remain in Sonora long?"

"Not long, not as long as Moses did in his desert. I decided to come to the U.S. myself, cross into the 'promised land', see if I could find my father and mother. Of course, I didn't find them, but it gave me another reason to keep moving.

"I've been running for years. I'm still doing it. I've had no peace, no rest. Always trying to stay ahead of him, that goddamn devil that seems to live in me somewhere. I can't do it anymore. He can have me now; there's nothing real left anyway. There hasn't been for years, just my will to keep moving on, but that's gone now, like the fucking water in that barrel. Nothing but bitter piss is left."

"Don't say that. It's too terrible to hear in this place."

"Yes, terrible but fitting. Now it's coming to a close. I must atone. I've run as far and as fast as I can, and nothing can drown out their voices, or his. The devil has found me and there is nowhere else to go."

*   *   *

There is something about movement that seems to heal and comfort. Once when I had a toothache, the pain so terrible that I could not even move my head, my mother could not sleep for thinking about me. She made my father take me in his truck for a ride. I remember that the motion, the feeling that we were going somewhere, that something was being done, made me forget my pain. When we returned home, I was asleep. That is how I felt when the train began to move. I forgot the heat and the smell of the dead men that by now was so powerful that even the stink of the urine-covered floors could not be detected. I had to keep myself from laughing. Texas by sun-up, I thought.

I tried to wake Berto to tell him we were moving and everything was going to be alright. But he didn't wake up. I kept shaking him even after I knew he was dead. I don't know how long I tried to revive him. I thought that if I gave him some water he would somehow be undead, but I was too afraid to try, in case Pablo might hear. He still sat undisturbed on his haystack.

I didn't want to sit next to Berto's body. I was afraid he would start to stink, and I didn't want to witness his decay. I took my bedroll and scooted as far as possible from the body.

And then I saw Pablo. He was standing up, holding the axe in front of him like a staff, then lifting it above his head, stretching his arms and back slowly. He looked up and a thin ray of sunlight lit his eyes. He seemed to be gaining strength from the stream of light, feeding on the heat that engulfed the car. He was illuminated, almost majestic. He smiled, baring his teeth, and as he opened his mouth I heard a roar. It surrounded me, and then I saw a flash like the lightning I had seen strike trees in the mountains of Bustamante. And then it was dark.

I heard the men around me squirming like snakes, panting and moaning. One begged for water. "A drop. A drop, please God, only a drop," he moaned. Then he began to curse

God. But soon he pleaded with God once more, his voice a pained groan full of anguish and resignation. It was terrible to hear.

Chico scraped the walls of the car, his skin coming away on the splintered planks. I could no longer resist the motion of the train, and I rolled back and forth. I thought I would vomit again but I didn't have the strength to heave. I felt a man's leg brush against my face. It smelled of urine. The man moaned in agony.

"My eye," he said. "God save me. God hear me."

I turned my face slowly, trying to get out of reach of his legs. I saw Pablo motionless above the writhing bodies, sitting on top of the haystack again. He seemed to be watching, his hand gripping the axe like a scepter.

*　　*　　*

"You don't have the strength to save your own life."

"I do."

"You don't. You brought with you all that you hoped to escape."

"No."

"Yes, even me."

"No."

"Estoy aquí. You brought me with you."

"Who are you then?"

"Tú sabes."

"Who?"

"Don't you recognize my voice? You heard it long ago in the dark."

"When? I don't remember."

"You couldn't move. You lay in fear listening for the whisper that turned your blood cold."

"Father?"

"You lay there unable to even shudder, so terrified you couldn't even turn your face."

"No."

"You could have moved. I beat you, wishing you would move."

"You locked me in the darkness, you bastard."

"No, you believed you were locked in the darkness."

"No, I remember. You left me there."

"I showed you how to get out."

"No."

"I taught you, but you failed."

"No."

"You failed."

"No!"

\*    \*    \*

I rolled on the floor in delirium. My tongue was swollen again, and from deep within I began to feel the sting of a scorpion. My neck was pierced by needles, the sensation spreading down my back and chest. My fingers dug into my skin, digging and tearing, trying to pull the itch away as if it were a thin wool shroud.

I could no longer open my eyes. The lids could not scrape across their dry surfaces. And yet in my delirium there was still a part of me that refused to writhe in agony. I knew I would soon be dead. I didn't remember Pablo, or the railroad car, or even my name. The train seemed to be moving, but then I would stop rolling on the floor and the stillness of the car pulled at me, held me to the floor, sucking at my back and legs, swallowing me. I turned as if in a scorching whirlwind. The huge door of the boxcar was blown open and light rushed in, surrounding me. The whirlwind lifted me, carrying me out into the daylight. Trees loomed overhead, but the sun's rays pierced the thick foliage. I looked up, shielding my eyes, and as I did I rose above the trees.

"Am I in heaven?" I asked.

I waited for an answer but heard only the wind. The sunlight that fell on my naked back began to concentrate between my shoulders. The ray of light grew smaller and hotter, like a thin beam of light focused through a magnifying glass. I tried to turn away from the burning stream, but it followed me. I thrashed as it scorched my back. My arm twisted at the shoulder, flapping as I tried to beat out the fire eating my flesh. I smelled my burning skin. I tried to dig out the charred flesh with my nails.

# Chapter Eleven

It was dark again, and I reached into the bedroll and took the canteen. I opened it and drank. The man next to me heard the water running into my mouth. He began to moan, sounding like a dying dog whimpering when it knows all is lost. His arms moved feebly, his fingers weakly outstretched like those of a starving beggar. He could do no more. The train's grunts drowned his sounds.

The water gushed into my mouth, soaking my tongue, running down my throat, flooding my empty stomach. I felt tears form in my eyes and my lids slowly opened. I took another drink, this time gulping sloppily, letting some of it trickle down my lips. Within minutes the itching stopped.

The man whimpering next to me was Alejandro. I looked at Pablo, who was still sitting on the bale of hay. He looked straight ahead but didn't seem to focus. I moved toward Alejandro slowly, keeping watch on Pablo as I did. Alejandro stopped moaning as I put a hand to his mouth. His lips were cracked and thick.

"Shhh," I whispered.

I raised his head. I poured a drink of water into his mouth. His tongue lapped loudly as it guided the drops down his throat.

"We have to kill him," he said finally.

"How can we kill him? We're dying of thirst, and you can't even get up. What will we defend ourselves with when the axe blade is tearing through the air? Do you have anything that can prevent his splitting your head?"

"My eye is rotting. I'll be dead soon, and when your water runs out you'll be fucking dead too."

"We may be in Texas in minutes. Why risk getting killed now?" I asked.

"Give me one more drink, I beg you. Please, my eye."

I gave Pablo another look. He had not moved. "If I give you another drink, you must tell me what you and Pablo planned with Rosales."

"Yes, I'll tell you everything I know, but give me the water first. I feel my tongue swelling again."

I put the canteen to his mouth. He put his hands over mine, pouring a long stream of water.

"Tell me," I said, pulling the canteen away.

"He's carrying a package. It's under the bale of hay. It's worth a lot. Someone is waiting for it when we arrive. We're to watch the men and make sure we get to Texas. Rosales told us that if we kept the men quiet, we would arrive safely. He told us the axe would be in the boxcar. He told us we would be overseers once we started work if we got that package to Houston safely. But that cabrón has gone crazy. Look at how he stares at nothing. He sits up on that bale as if in judgment, like a fucking mayor. Look at my eye. It's poisoning me. I would gouge it out if it would end this misery. He could end this misery!" he said, pointing at Pablo.

"Look at that fucker. He doesn't seem to be weakening. He hasn't even moved. He sits up straight, waiting for another execution. I should have killed him, but my eye is ruined." He turned back to me. I could see that his eye was puffed and running. I imagined I could smell it. "You. It's got to be you that kills him. Then you could save us all. You can break down the door with the axe. I can't help you with my body, but I'll help you make a plan."

"No," I said.

"You will save us all."

"All I'll do is get killed. If you lie quietly I'll give you a drink of water every time I take one. We can survive if we just wait. We'll be in Texas soon. We've been in this car long enough to have walked there."

"But my eye," Alejandro said too loudly.

"Your eye won't kill you as quickly as Pablo will."

"What good did it do your friend to wait?" he asked.

I moved away from him and sat against the wall. Turning my head, I looked at Berto's body. I knew he was rotting, but the stench of decay in the box was so strong that I couldn't tell if he had started to smell.

"How would we kill him?" I asked.

"I can't help you kill him physically. I'm too weak. I can't even see. But I'll help you to get him close enough so you can jump on him. He'll be watching me and you can come from behind. Take his axe and split his spine. You've been resting and you've had water. He'll be no match for you if you surprise him."

"How are you going to get him over here?"

"I'll call him. I'll tell him that Rosales told me something only I know. That maldito will want to hear what it is."

"Call him then."

"Pablo," Alejandro said, "you're making a mistake by letting us die."

Pablo didn't seem to hear. "Rosales sent us to die. I haven't told you the plans he made with me. Are you listening?"

Pablo stayed motionless.

"Don't you want to hear what he was planning for you? All for the money. He knows about you. He told me you were a pendejo for cheating him. That I was going to be his new man."

Pablo turned his head slightly.

"Are you deaf?" cried Alejandro. "I'm dying and I want to tell you what's waiting for you, you son of a bitch. You think you're smart hiding those drugs, thinking you've figured out how to make money on this trip. Rosales has got a plan for you, you fucking shit. I won't be able to help now, but it's waiting for you when you step off this train.

"He found out about you, carnal. Guess who told him? Rosales doesn't like being cheated. You know that, right? You remember Santos? You helped take care of him. Well, what we have planned for you is worse. I'm as good as dead, but I want you to know you're getting yours soon."

Pablo said quietly, "I'd be doing you a favor if I caved in your worthless skull. If I believed what you're saying it would be better to watch you claw your own eye out than to kill you myself. You think I give a shit about any plans you made with Rosales? You were the first one I thought I'd have to kill, but that poor bastard's finger put you down. Rosales's plans have no place here, they've withered away in this heat. You think his word means a goddamn thing? When I walk out of here and you're just another rotting corpse, no one is going to see me again. Rosales better pray I don't come across him, that fat bastard. I'd love to have him here, watching him squirm like you. You're both weak. Your plan . . . Your plans haven't come to much, have they? They're as dead as you. Lie down and die, perrito." Pablo turned calmly away.

Alejandro spoke, perhaps to me. "And my family?"

I didn't reply. I was feeling very tired now. The anticipation had left me fatigued. I tried to sleep.

"And my family?" he said again, this time louder, as if he expected the men around him to give him the answer. "My family," he said more urgently. He spoke as if it were only now occurring to him that he was going to die, that his family would be left alone.

"Go to sleep," I said. "Your family will be alright. We'll be at work soon. Then you can bring them over. You can at least send them money."

"No," he said, panic in his voice. "No. They will be alone now." He gripped my hand tightly. "I will be dead soon, don't you understand?" He did not release me.

I thought about my own mother. "Maybe you shouldn't have come. Now they're alone," I said, remembering her face the day I'd left.

"You have to help me," he cried, his voice rising in desperation. "You have to kill Pablo. They'll die."

Pablo was watching us now.

"Be quiet," I said. "Lie still. We'll be there soon. Sleep. Close your eyes and rest." I looked at Pablo, who was still staring at us. He focused on me now. He seemed to smile. His lips did not curl, yet he was amused.

"Please," pleaded Alejandro, "kill him."

I took his hand from my shoulder. "Don't be an idiot," I said. "Shhh."

"Mi gente," he said again softly. "The water. Offer him the water."

"You're delirious," I said. "Be quiet before you get us killed."

"He'll set us free for the water. Don't you see? Ask him. Ask him!"

I looked up at Pablo. He stared into my face and smiled. "What's that fool crying about?"

Alejandro didn't wait for me to answer. "He has water," he said. "He'll give it to you. See, I'll do you a favor and you'll do us a favor." He said to me, "Give him the water, you. Give him the water so he'll get us out of here."

"Yes," said Pablo, "give me the water so I can let you out of here." He was still smiling.

"He's delirious," I said. "If I had water, I sure as hell wouldn't have given him any. I wouldn't be lying here dying of thirst. He's crazy."

"Yes, he does," cried Alejandro. "He gave me some just a few minutes ago. You see, Pablo, I want us to survive. I'm helping you."

Pablo stood. "Maybe you're also suffering from delirium," he said to me. "It's possible you don't remember. If you did have water, you certainly would have told me about it. I saw how you treated the old man. You're a humanitarian. I can tell you're a sharer." He walked toward us.

"Yes," said Alejandro, "he has it in his bedroll. Get it from him, Pablo. See, I'm still your partner."

Pablo was coming closer. I reached into my bedroll and pulled out the canteen. I unscrewed the cap and began to pour water into my mouth. It lasted only a second. The haft of the axe hit the side of my head. The blow was enough to knock me backward. The canteen fell on the floor, some of the water spilling onto the wooden planks.

Pablo picked it up quickly, springing out of reach before I could sit up. The blow had been strong enough to make me dizzy, and blood poured from a long cut that ran across my ear. I thought I would throw up again, but instead I fainted.

# Chapter Twelve

It was true—I had been forsaken. I was in hell. It was hot, as the priest in Bustamante had said. All around me I could hear other lost souls squirming in pain, but I couldn't see them. The priest had been wrong about the fire. There was no fire, no light, just the heat and the demons that would not leave me alone. They pulled, poked, and shook me, not content to leave me alone in my suffering. . . .

My mother was trying to wake me. I was in my bed and would not stir. I was being stubborn about going to breakfast. Was it Sunday?

I saw a white, bony hand. I followed the hand with my eyes to a white face with large black holes for eyes and a large black hole for a mouth. The skinless fingers poked at me, and the hole of the mouth grew larger until it closed around me and death swallowed me whole.

It wasn't death. It was Alejandro who shook me. My eyes opened slowly. It was completely dark in the box now. For a moment I thought the blow had made me blind.

"Wake up," Alejandro pleaded. "He's not going to help us. We have to kill him. Listen to me. Wake up."

I pushed him away from me. He fell backwards without a sound. The movement sent a wave of pain crashing through my head. I felt dizzy again. The pain almost made me scream, but I knew that screaming would only make it worse. I concentrated on staying still. Little by little the pounding lessened. I tried to turn my head slowly, but a cold spike pierced my eyes and I stopped.

Alejandro had sat back up. "You have to convince him," he said. "Tell him we gave him the water. Tell him we must survive." He made a move toward me.

"Stay back or I'll kill you myself," I said. Pain ran from my jaw to the back of my skull. I felt myself falling.

He stayed back. He put his face into his arms and began to cry. I think if I had been able to move, I would have killed him. I would have tried to rip his head from his shoulders, sticking my thumb into his rotting eye, pulling it from his head like a tomato. But I could not, and the anger made the pain worse. Instead I closed my eyes. I had not even thought about Pablo.

*    *    *

"Always pray," my mother's voice reminded me. "If you pray, God hears you and sends angels to minister to you. God is faithful even when you're not." I heard her but couldn't believe her.

"What about my father?" I asked her. "He's dead. Why didn't God do anything to stop it?"

"Your father isn't really dead," she answered. "His soul lives on. Your heavenly father looks down on you and sees your heart, your pain, and your confusion. Put your trust in Him. He is the only father you need, and He'll be with you everywhere you go if only you maintain your faith. You do that by praying and believing even when you can't see a way."

I wondered if God saw me now. I certainly couldn't see Him or feel Him. I tried to pray, but I felt foolish, and the smell of that box corrupted my thoughts. I knew that like that stench, my prayers would go no higher than the ceiling. My faith would not transcend those walls. I couldn't even blame Him. Who'd want to be looking down into this foul box? I wasn't his son anymore. I felt that. God's eyes were no longer on me.

"Your father, now that he's in heaven, will always be able to hear you, too. When he was on earth, if you needed him, he was sometimes too far away to help or even to hear your voice. When you feel alone, search your heart and listen carefully, and you'll hear him. You'll hear a small, still voice, if only you listen."

In that box I heard nothing but my own raspy breathing.

*   *   *

When I awoke, he was staring at me. "You know why I didn't kill you?" he asked.

I tried not to move. I was hoping that if I kept very still he would think I was still unconscious. But it was no use.

"It's because I thought you were already dead. Why waste energy on a corpse? When I saw you wake up, I was surprised, but I was not concerned enough to walk over and finish you off. You'll be dead soon enough, just like that maldito next to you."

I looked at Alejandro. He was dead. His good eye was closed, but the rotted eye was puffed open, its shiny blackness staring upward.

"You killed him?" I asked.

"He wasn't worth the effort. It was better to see him suffer."

"You think you're going to watch me die too, then," I said.

"I'm going to watch you all die. I think you're the only one left alive in any case. But yes, I'll watch you die. I'll drink your water and watch you die from the lack of it."

*   *   *

"What if I were to tell you that there is nothing outside this box? No trees, no grass, no sky, no life. Nada, ni madre. All that exists is this box," he said.

"I wouldn't believe you."

"What could you do to prove me a liar? You've been in this car so long, how do you know that what existed out there when you entered is still out there? Perhaps you've been riding in circles. Maybe you're only hearing voices. Look at the corpse of the old man. Doesn't it resemble you? Perhaps you're viewing your future."

He waited for me to reply. I said nothing.

"Perhaps it would be better to kill you. It would save you. You would be spared from knowing what does or does not wait for you. You don't really want to know. You would rather I do you such a favor? ¿Te salvo, mijito?"

I looked at the canteen, which sat at his feet. Moisture glistened in a ray of light. Had there been any men still alive they would have licked the floor for that moisture. Pablo read my mind.

"Those dogs licked the puddles of their piss. This would have made them weep for joy. Did you see them become animals? Begging me to save them, asking that I open another's veins so they could prolong the end. Qué pendejada. They wanted to extend the length of their suffering. They clung to life so long they ended by hating it. Why? Did they hope they would be rescued? By whom?"

He listened for my answer. My head still pounded from the blow, but I had managed to drag myself to the wall on Pablo's right. He didn't seem to notice.

"Who would want to rescue such cowardly creatures? I won't do them the honor of calling them dogs. Even dogs exhibit bravery at times. No, they acted like the worst animal, a human. I sat here on top of this bale, watching them. They moaned and cried, dragging themselves through the mierda. Filthy. They became cannibals. You saw them. They returned to their infancies when their mothers suckled them, knowing nothing, feeling only blind instinct. Did you see them, sucking the blood from each other, drinking urine. I laughed because I knew them for what they were. They were scared rats, slimy, frothing at the mouth, turning on each other in the dark. The stench of rotting carcasses penetrated their pretense of being human.

"No one did anything when I killed that delirious animal. Cobardes. Every man wanted him dead. Inside his heart, every man thanked me for doing what he would have done had he the courage. I'm sure many of them told themselves I was brutal and vicious. They soothed their consciences with the knowledge that I alone drove the axe into his head. And when they were thirsty and insane with heat they came to me, begging for me to break the door down for them, even when the axe lay on the floor and they could easily have taken it from me. 'Save us,' they cried to me like I was a priest or medicine man, when I was as weak as they physically and only one man."

The train stopped moving.

"I'm the only man in this car. I'm the only human. They recognized this. They feared me and I'm still alive. They saw I had no fear in me. I don't fear this darkness because I know that darkness exists out there too. It seeps into this box. It comes from out there, not from inside. We're not trapped in darkness. This box is only a replica of what is true outside. What difference does it make to me where I spend my time in the dark? In here I know where I am in the darkness; out there no one can ever be certain. Isn't it much better to know where you are? If these men had known the darkness that waited for them on the other side of the door, they would have flung themselves on this axe, giving thanks as the blade tore through their miserable hearts." Pablo held the axe away from his body, as if men were lining up to fall upon it.

He opened the canteen and took a drink. "Do you know who I am?" he asked me.

I said nothing. The itching was beginning again.

"I asked you who I am. Answer me," he demanded.

"The old man told me you were the devil," I said.

"No," Pablo began, "but close enough. I've finished in Mexico. I've killed many men for profit. I've learned how to feed off fear and blame. I've spent my life preparing to go where I will be rewarded. And you idiots shake your fists at God and curse at the devil for your misfortunes. I don't. I'm my own God and my own devil. I suffer only at my own hands, and for my triumphs I praise only myself."

"Berto knew," I said.

"He knew nothing. He died passively. He lost. Everyone in this train has had to contend with me, and I have won every time."

"You *are* the devil," I said.

"Your devil has only to be named and he appears. He's willing to carry the burden of blame because in return he gets life—he gets the accuser's strength and freedom. I must admit it's not a bad thing to be the devil. These dead gave me their souls so they could die blameless to themselves. I've accepted their sacrifice and will live."

I started to scratch again. Blood and skin soon covered my hands.

"It seems you're in need of water," said Pablo. "I will do you the favor of withholding it. You'll enter eternity faultless, another victim of the unholy one."

"You'll die too," I said.

"No. I recognize the power of evil. I didn't come on this trip to escape the grasp of the devil, daring to imagine that there existed a place outside his kingdom. I came for a new opportunity. I hadn't been in this car two hours before I realized that I had already been rewarded for my search. Here were twelve men who were willing to make me their devil. They made this box hell and I became its prince. They gave me their blood, their hate, their lives, and their visions. What else could a devil desire? I'm already successful.

"I'm like Cortés. He had the courage to burn his ships. Imagine how the weak ones cringed when he took that torch and one by one set fire to the ships. They must have been ragged, scared, homesick. All of them hating themselves for taking that impossible journey. They were hungry and lost, too. And here was this madman setting fire to the only means of returning! But no one dared to stop him. They recognized that here was someone who was prepared to journey to the end, even into death. Even death must respect that. A whole fucking empire in the hands of one man and a few hundred half-men. I have the same resolution, the same strength, and the same hardness.

"No one will write about me. You're the only witness left. Until you die, you'll give me the gift of history."

Through the dim light I could see Pablo smiling. He put the axe in his lap and ran his finger along its blade.

"They were scared," I said. "There's no evil in that. They died because they wanted to finish the journey. They died hoping. There's no evil in hope."

He stepped off the bale of hay, standing shakily, using the axe as a staff. He took the canteen, opened it quickly, and drank the rest of the water. "You have just named the foulest of the two sins," he said, flinging the canteen behind him. "It is hope and fear that allow evil to exist and grow. Fools believe hate and greed are the precursors of evil. They're wrong. Hope allows the weak to continue in weakness, to revel in it. It makes them feel noble. Hope is for the meek, for children holding hands in the dark, for the condemned man, for those who have nothing. They pacify their yearnings and their inadequacies with hope. When a father sees his child dying of hunger and he accuses himself of cowardice, of being less than a man, he finds the delusion of hope. He tries to hide in hope. He dies in hope. I am powerful because I recognize the futility of hope and the power of evil." Pablo banged the axe on the floor for emphasis.

"I still have hope," I said.

"Look at yourself. You're dying. Your skin is peeling. Blood pours from your wounds and pus flows down your fingers.

Your tongue is swollen and black. You no longer have enough water in your body to sweat. In an hour you'll start shaking and scourge what remains of your flesh with your nails. You'll beg me to kill you. But you won't be able to speak. Your mind will scream out to me, but you'll only be able to groan. And even that will be agony as your throat cracks. You'll hope for your death. Perhaps I'll take mercy and become the angel of death for you. But I don't think so. I think I'll bend down very low, low enough to stare into your dry eyes. I'll feed on your misdirected hate. I'll see when, at the moment of your death, you realize you should have used your hate much earlier. I'll grow stronger in that hate. Then I'll break from this train and go and find others, hope-filled others."

Pablo walked back to the bale. He kept his back to me and stood expectantly.

"My father wasn't afraid," I said.

"Then he didn't teach you well," Pablo said without turning.

"He tried to teach me," I said.

"He failed. You failed also, or you would not be in this box. You would have stayed in your home and faced what you ran from. You faced fear and didn't know it came from within. You thought you could run from it, but you brought it with you. Is that what your father taught you? To run from your fears?"

I didn't say anything. I waited for my father to speak to me. I searched my memories, hoping to find a word that did not sound foolish even to me. Even in my mind I saw nothing but the darkness that surrounded me. And I remembered the dread my father could not help me define or overcome. His words of encouragement and strength were lost to me. As I strained to hear them, their echoes drowned in the darkness.

"You can no longer speak," Pablo said.

I said nothing.

"Your tongue is too swollen? Are you choking on your last utterance? Do the words of hope and faith feel dry in your throat? You can't force them. You're too close to death. Perhaps death is whispering something to you, telling you that hell is much nearer than you think. It's very near. It's in you and around you at this moment. You're seeing truth now." He turned to face me. "But you shouldn't feel cheated. You're one of the elect. You've been allowed to see truth before death. Very few men are chosen. Do you see the truth? It's right there in front of you. It's reaching for you. Don't you feel it? Its fingers are outstretched, its message written on its dark face. Open your eyes and see it. This is your last opportunity."

Pablo approached me, slowly raising the axe.

"I still have the strength to resist you," I said.

He stopped, lowering the axe. "You don't need strength to resist me. You need strength to resist yourself. It won't be much longer before your strength is gone, and then you will whimper, begging for death, but I may not want you dead at that moment."

I tried to pray again, this time giving thanks, but no still voice spoke to me and no answer came, no light, no vision, only the darkness that now seemed to live in me.

# Chapter Thirteen

In the morning I woke quickly, stretching my arms high above my head, reaching for the white ceiling of the tent. Bright light filtered through the fabric. My fingers could almost but not quite touch the ceiling. Outside the tent I heard the workers picking and plucking, tearing fruit from the trees and pulling vegetables from the ground. Footsteps sounded close, thudding, dragging, sometimes clinking faintly. I fumbled for the flap. I could still hear them outside. And then silence. I stared at the ceiling and the light dimmed, but there were no shadows. I watched, forgetting that I was looking for the flap. From far away came a sound like cowbells heard at dusk through an April wind from a distant pasture. I listened as the sound faded away. I looked up again, and the ceiling was black. Then I awoke, the ceiling was white again and the noise of the work outside mixed with wind. I was aware of time passing quickly, the light growing fainter as I sat thinking about its passing. The wind subsided and, looking up at the ceiling of the tent, I saw that it was night. The workers had grown silent again, and I hadn't looked for the flap. The ceiling was white once more and I knew I had to find the flap and not be distracted again. My hands ran over smooth sides, seamless and cool, with no flaps or edges. I felt along the floor and sides, all but the ceiling which I couldn't reach.

I stopped to listen.

This time only the breeze, and then a sound almost gone by the time it reached me, the wind taking it away before I could understand it. My hands searched feverishly. The darkness slowly stained the whiteness of the ceiling as my hands moved faster, the fingers dragging across the smooth walls. A bell rang under the hoarse whisper of the wind, "Stand up . . . ." The voice trailed off, the rest of its message lost.

*   *   *

I awoke scraping the walls. Berto lay at my feet, his dead eyes looking away from me. I wanted to close them, to keep them from staring, but I could not.

"You wound up very close to your friend," said Pablo. "You thrashed and rolled around in your sleep until you found a resting place alongside the old man. That's very interesting. I think you know it's almost over. You're selecting your burial ground and the one you will share it with."

Pablo no longer sat upright. He leaned against the wall, the axe under his legs as if he were afraid it might be stolen.

"You've been asleep," I said.

"No, I've been watching you," said Pablo. "I see how weak you've become. It's no longer necessary to hold up the axe. Why waste energy on the dead?"

"Your voice," I said. "It's different. You sound tired, as if you're fighting to stay awake. You are tired."

"If I thought you were still dangerous to me, I would have killed you while you moaned in your sleep. Maybe I should have. But there's no point in killing a dead man."

"Why did you come?" I asked.

He said nothing.

"Remember," I said, "I'm already dead. You're speaking to a corpse. I'm no longer dangerous. If that's true, then tell me why you came."

He shifted slowly but with purpose, a predator aware of prey. He took the axe from under his legs, placing its head on his right forearm. "I'm bringing something with me," he said, "something Rosales is sending to the Americans. He entrusted me with it." He stopped. The midday air was sapping his strength, but he didn't lean back again. He stayed rigid, even while the motion of the train swayed his body from side to side.

\*   \*   \*

The light illuminating the ceiling of the tent woke me. It was not as bright as before. Outside, the wind shook the trees, drowning out sounds. There were no footsteps, no voices, no sound except for the wind. Already the ceiling was dimming. The time of brightness shortened each day. I listened, too tired to struggle to find the flap. A bell rang. It was so faint I thought it might be my imagination.

"What is that bell?" I wondered. "Have all the workers gone?" The wind squalled, shaking the walls of the tent.

Maybe it's better I don't find my way out there. They may have already left and the wind sounds too strong.

I heard the bell again. I wondered if that was the workers.

"Stand up." The wind twisted the words so they sounded as if they came from across a canyon during a storm. I wondered if I had really heard them. Maybe they had been a trick of the wind, a whistle that I formed into meaning.

\*   \*   \*

"Stand up." The words stayed with me even after I awoke. I did not know what they meant, or from where they came.

The heat was killing me.

I'm dying now, I thought. I won't wake up next time I fall asleep. I no longer had the strength to scratch myself. The desire to claw and dig out the itch was not powerful enough for me to raise my arms.

I looked at Pablo. He was collapsed against the wall, scraping his arms against it.

"Why don't you use your axe?" I said. "It will be much quicker. It will stop the itch."

He stopped.

"You're dying, too," I said. "It won't be long until you're lying on the floor next to your dead friend. I'm looking at a corpse."

"Shut your mouth," he said. "Shut your mouth or I'll kill you. I'll open your skull."

You can't do it, I thought. You're too weak now, Pablo. The hate and blood you fed off is gone. I don't have the strength to hate you, and the others are dead. They're beyond such things. It's over, and you didn't win anything. When they open this box, they'll find thirteen corpses, and one of them will be next to the door, holding an axe in decaying hands.

"They'll wonder why you didn't break the doors down," I said. "They won't know that you tried, that you crawled to the doors, dragging yourself through half-rotted corpses, across a blood-soaked floor, through dried urine, your face distorted from the effort, the scorching air torturing your parched throat. They won't have seen you as you reached the door, drained, holding your breath from the pain. They won't have seen your weak attempts to pull yourself to your feet. You'll fall as you get onto your knees. You'll lie on the floor, no longer able to breathe, gasping the burning air, moaning, dying."

"Why don't you get up and take this axe then?" he said suddenly. "If I'm too weak now, save yourself. All you have to do is stand up, walk over here, and snatch the axe from my hands. If I'm so weak, I'll sit here feebly, begging you to kill me before you break free. I'll make it easy for you. I'll lie here as you raise the axe. I'll be anyone you want me to be. I'm the one who murdered the old man, the one who took your water, who with pleasure watched the men die. Who else do you hate? Oh, yes, I'm the devil, the father you're running from. I'm the rotting mierda your family eats every night, the seeping pus infection your little brother had on his foot when he stepped on a piece of glass. I'm the doctor your family prayed would come while your little brother mumbled in a fever. Come kill me. Can you? Perhaps I'm not as weak as you think."

"You're as weak as I am, Pablo. I don't have the strength. If I did I would break free."

The train swerved, grinding against the rail.

"You're afraid, a coward like the rest. You never had the strength," he said.

\*     \*     \*

The ceiling was yellow. It no longer turned white but alternated between black and pale yellow.

The wind groaned against the walls of the tent. I pretended to search with my hands, tracing the walls with my fingers, never moving beyond the area where I knew I would not find the flap. I didn't want to leave. The wind was terrible. I was afraid that once outside, the wind would pick me up and blow me away, far away, across the dirt plains, the rows of corn fanning far beneath me. I would fall, the wind cruelly picking me up just before I hit the trees, then dropping me again, my legs flailing, my hands grasping for what was not there, and again dropping, only to be lifted up for another fall.

But now the wind threatened my tent. It shook the walls, ready to rip them to pieces and snatch me up, I rootless, picked up like a leaf, then crushed. The wind terrified me, keeping me in the tent for protection, yet promising destruction if I stayed.

And the ones out there had left. I no longer heard them. They did not pick anymore. Maybe the wind had blown them away, the ones I longed to join, that I heard outside my tent, walking, picking, and pulling. I would not find them. It was dark out there now. The ceiling of the tent proved it. I would get lost looking for them now. They had left me here. Now if I left the tent, even if I withstood the wind, I would get lost in the dark, never finding them, wandering around listening for the bell that would mean they were near. But the bell would be drowned out by the wind, and I would wander in the blindness of the dark, in the deafness of the roar of the wind.

Better to stay in the tent. My hands still searched, more slowly now, in case I found the flap. If I found it I might try. So my fingers felt the walls to find what I must not and yet must find. Around, across the top, across the bottom, behind me, and in front.

\* \* \*

I sat up. My fingers were covered with splinters. The train had stopped. I began to pull the splinters from my fingers. Some of them were so small I tried to use my teeth. My lips were large bleeding blisters. I felt them tearing as I opened my mouth to grasp a splinter. The blood seeped onto my tongue. The taste nauseated me, and the burning pain forced me to close my mouth slowly. I dropped my hands and left the splinters alone.

I can't even crawl, I thought, or use my mouth to pull a splinter from my finger.

Pablo's mouth was open, his tongue hanging out. He moaned lowly, one hand covering his groin, the other gripping the axe handle.

I stared at the axe. You can't even pull a splinter from your hand, I thought, and you think you can pull an axe from his hands and still have the strength to break open the boxcar door. That is ridiculous.

My legs felt heavy and stiff, like fallen trees. I could not make them move. I thought about death. I didn't think it could be worse than this. It would be better, a relief. There would be no heat or stench, and the pain would stop. But the darkness. I would remain in darkness, stiff, unable to move. I would rot. I didn't want to die, but I couldn't move.

"It's your coffin."

"You're dead."

"You were never born."

I closed my eyes to silence the voices. The dim light inside the box seemed to be trapped. I did not see anything of my old life, any pictures of my mother or father or home. I saw only more darkness. It was inside me now, around me. I was darkness.

So this is death, I thought. I drifted, my body's heaviness dropping away from me as easily as a shoe might drop from a tired man's foot. I rested. I let the darkness fill my mind, feeling, seeing, and being nothing.

# Chapter Fourteen

M y father's voice.

"It's simple. Stand up." The wind had quieted long enough for me to hear his voice.

"I can't stand up," I said, but the wind once again began to roar. "I can't stand up," I yelled, the wind pulling the words away from my own ears.

Why can't I stand up? I thought.

The wind tugged at the tent now. It was ready to yank the stakes from the ground.

If I could find the flap, I thought.

The ceiling of the tent was yellow with pale light filtering through it. But there was no flap. There were no seams, no openings. It was smooth, made of strong material. If the wind could not tear it down, how could I?

The light was growing dimmer, was disappearing. Shadows appeared. And then through the wind, from far away, very faintly, I heard a bell.

Was it them?

Were they close?

Would I see them?

I lifted my hands again, but they did not reach the ceiling. Slowly, I stood. Again I raised my hands. My fingers touched the ceiling. I thrust them through the material. My fingers pushed open holes. It was just paper. The wind was thundering against paper. The ceiling fell apart. I pulled myself through, shading my eyes from the brightness of the sunlight.

I was in a field that extended to the horizon in the east and west, to mountains in the north, and to the ocean in the south. There was silence. The wind had stopped. The few scattered trees were motionless, the air both cool and dry and warm and wet.

They were standing in two rows. There were many people, all dressed in white, all wearing straw hats. They didn't move as they stared at the ground. They stooped down, and I heard the bell. But it wasn't a bell; it was the sound of the chains around their ankles. My father was among them. And Berto.

*   *   *

The train jerked noisily, waking me as I held onto the wall. It was beginning to move again, but the motion didn't comfort me as it had before. As the train started forward, swaying, rolling me back and forth in the black, I didn't know if I was really awake.

Am I in the dream?

Is that the wind I hear?

Is this the tent?

I fell back against the wall, feeling the rough planks of wood. It stung, but I forced my hands to sweep across the boards. This wasn't the dream. I wore no chains.

You wear no chains.

No, I'm free to die.

I looked at Pablo. He sat in the same position, still leaning against the wall, still grasping the axe.

"Speak to me," I said.

He said nothing. He sat rigidly, saying all he had needed to say.

"Speak to me, you son of a bitch," I yelled. "Cabrón, tell me something."

"I have said everything."

"More!"

He was silent. He had told me all.

I pressed against the wall, closing my eyes then opening them, scared. It was there, all around me now: more than the darkness, more than the black, more than even the death and rot I lay with. It was no longer calling me; it had found me. My eyes stayed open still, the terror forcing me to watch, the cowardice begging me not to.

I pressed against the wall, trying to go inside it, through it. But the evil had me now and there was nowhere left to go. I felt cold stroke my neck; the heat of the day now longed for. My back was sweaty, and the cold blew across it, fingers playing with my flesh, tickling, nudging, as if teasing a sleepy child.

It whispered to me, promising to wake me from the dream. "Come now," it said almost gently.

I cringed, pulling away, pushing into the wall. "No," I cried, turning my face against the splintered boards.

"Come now," it said hoarsely, its mouth on my neck, opening, licking my skin slowly, tasting me.

Then it was silent, motionless, still holding me by the neck. After a moment it said, "Come now."

"No." I pulled myself up, turning my face into the darkness. I tried to stand, and I felt its heavy hands upon my shoulders, pushing me down. I resisted, forcing my legs to lift, my hands pressing against the wall. I stumbled, my knees shaking, my head swaying in and out of blackness.

Slowly my hips came up from the floor. My hands fought to balance me against the wall.

Still leaning, I rose, my arms inching farther up until I felt my legs unfold completely, the muscles in my thighs stretching, my knees locking as I stood. I leaned against the wall, feeling as if the next movement of the train would send me crashing back to the floor. My lungs shriveled, unable to suck in the burning air. I concentrated on staying on my feet, relying on the wall for support, rolling with the train's motions.

Pablo had not moved, and now as I watched him, he remained motionless.

I thrust myself from the wall and pitched forward. I reached behind and grasped the planks of wood, steadying myself.

He's too far away, I thought. Sit back down and rest.

I felt myself sag, the muscles in my legs melting.

No, I won't get back up.

Rest. Sit back down. Sleep. Lie down until you are ready to struggle again.

My knees buckled, my calves trembling as I felt the tendons in my feet strain. My back began to slide down the wall. Heavy hands again pressed on my shoulders.

I pushed back. Slowly I stood straight again. I looked at Pablo, still motionless. I focused on the axe cradled in his arms.

From within I heard, "He will kill you." I forced myself away from the wall, standing, anticipating the motion of the train. I watched him for a hint of movement, an uncurling of the hand, a twitch of the face, a roll of a shoulder. I stepped forward. I did not breathe. I made no sound. I waited for him to open his eyes, waited for the leap as he swung the axe into my face. But he didn't move.

I waited for courage, for the moment when I would rush forward blindly, screaming and beating him with my fists. But courage did not come. I watched him instead. And then I looked at the door. Light shone through the cracks. I moved forward again.

"I'm coming," I said.

I reached him running, a new energy racing through my tired legs. My hands grasped the axe and I pulled it free. He didn't resist. He didn't even open his eyes. He lay there, motionless and stiff, one hand still covering his crotch.

I asked myself, "How long? How long was I afraid of a corpse?"

How much had I imagined or hallucinated? Maybe since I had resisted, death had taken him instead. I felt weak again.

The running had drained me. The power that had surged through me as I prepared to kill him was now gone. I felt like a disappointed child. I had been prepared to kill my devil, only now I could not find him. I thought my devil was Pablo, but he was dead. Where had he gone?

Now I had only to break out of the box. I sat on the bale, Pablo's body supine on the floor. I looked for strength inside myself, but all I found was languor. I looked for words, but my mind was empty.

And so I stood. I walked to the door of the box, thinking of nothing. I lifted the axe for nothing and struck the door down. I felt nothing as the sunlight covered me, lit the car, the corpses, the brown interior. I threw the axe out of the car.

The train was moving slowly. I found the canteen lying a few feet from Pablo's body. I picked it up, slinging it over my head. I was not thinking. I was not looking for words of instruction. I walked to where the door had been. Flashes of green, beyond that a blue horizon and painful light. I shielded my eyes with my hand, forcing myself to look. The colors were brighter than I had imagined in the car. The trees opened their arms. I felt the air, fresh, new, and clean rushing over my face and through my hair. Beyond the trees I saw the sunlight reflected on a river, the light rippling over the fresh water. The water pulled me and I jumped, landed on my feet for just a moment, then toppled onto my back, over my head, then again, and again, blues, greens, the sky, now the trees, until finally, rolling to a stop, I lay on my back staring up, preparing to stand. Starting over now, not caring where.

## DATE DUE

| | | | |
|---|---|---|---|
| | | | |
| | | | |
| | | | |
| | | | |
| | | | |
| | | | |
| | | | |
| | | | |
| | | | |
| | | | |
| | | | |
| | | | |
| | | | |
| | | | |
| | | | |
| | | | |
| | | | |

HIGHSMITH